Hush

JUST THIS ONCE SERIES

DEBORAH BLADON

Also by Deborah Bladon

Chapter 1

Evan

"I'm not a coward. I am not a coward." A soft, smooth feminine voice catches me off guard.

I turn toward it and grab a quick glimpse of what looks like the world's most perfect ass in a pair of black lace panties. They vanish the second the woman in question stands upright again, the red umbrella in her hand mangled from the brutal wind.

"You don't strike me as a coward, sweetheart." I raise my near-empty glass of bourbon in a mock toast because any person brave enough to venture out in January in a New York City blizzard, dressed like it's the middle of July, deserves a medal. This one earns bonus points for having an ass that can halt a snowstorm in its path.

That may or may not be a fact, but the timing is sure as hell spot-on.

The deluge of snow that has blanketed the city for the past five hours has stopped abruptly. That wasn't the case up until a minute ago when I was standing, alone, outside this hotel contemplating what my next move will be.

Big picture stuff, not which-of-my-casual-hook-ups-should-I-call-tonight stuff.

"Thanks, stranger." She smooths her hands over the short skirt of her frilly navy blue dress as she takes in the length of my six-foot plus frame. "I'm not your sweetheart, though."

Wheat blonde hair, warm hazel eyes, glossy full pink lips, and an attitude.

Forget the big picture. My next move needs to involve this woman.

My eyes don't leave her angelic face even though I want to trail my gaze and my mouth over every inch of her body. "Fair enough. Introduce yourself, and while you're at it, I'd love to meet your imaginary friend too."

I can't resist the urge to look when her nipples pebble into hard points beneath the airy fabric of her dress. As much as I want that reaction to be from the rich baritone of my voice, I suspect it's from the burst of wind that just picked up her skirt. There's a brief flash of sheer lace covering smooth skin before she yanks the hem of the skirt back in place.

My evening just got a whole hell-of-a-lot better.

"My imaginary friend?" She tucks a piece of her windswept hair behind her ear. My fist clenches in envy. I want those waves balled in my hand so tightly that the only noise she makes is one that tells me she wants my cock deeper.

I crack a smile. "You were hell bent on convincing someone that you're not a coward. Since we're the only two out here and there's no phone in your hand, I take it that your imaginary friend is the asshole who thinks you're a coward. I'll argue your case if you point me in his direction, or is it her direction?"

"Are you a lawyer?"

I'll be anything she wants me to be. I'm a surgeon, vascular to be precise, and I have to be. Tonight, I don't want to be Dr. Evan Scott. I'd rather be the star of her future fantasies; that one awe-inspiring lay all women look back on for the rest of their life when they get themselves off.

"Not guilty." I hold my hand up in mock surrender. "Your name, beautiful. What is it?"

Her thickly lashed eyes widen as the heavy metal awning above us creaks under the weight of the wet snow. "It's Jane. Jane Smith."

She's the third *Jane Smith* I've met this month.

I'm not offended that the name offered is as fake as the smile plastered on the face of the doorman who is watching our every move from the warm comfort of the lobby. Experience has taught me that women in this town hide behind a false persona for just three reasons.

One is that their wedding ring is tucked in a pocket or a purse and they don't want the night to seep into their two kids, bake sales, walking the dog in the park, day-to-day life.

For the record, I avoid those women at all costs. They're easy to spot, even if they think they're fooling everyone, including themselves.

The second reason women morph into Jane Smith, Jane Doe or just plain Jane is they're prepping to hand over a fake number.

Eye contact is everything, and if a woman I'm after can't make it with me, I tap out. There are too many women on this island who are interested in what I'm offering. I'm not into wasting my time on someone whose type isn't tall with dark brown hair, blue eyes, muscular pecs, that cut V that women dream of, and a thick nine-inch cock.

Yeah, I measured. Every man does. He's a fucking liar if he doesn't admit it.

The third reason is why my new blonde friend tossed out the name Jane Smith to me just now. She's looking for the same thing I am. One night of no-personal-details, uninhibited, I-dare-you-to-walk-straight-after-that fucking.

"It's nice to meet you, Jane." I extend a hand because in public I'm always the perfect gentleman.

She takes a step forward, dragging her sorry looking umbrella behind her. Her hand lands in mine for a soft shake. It's just enough pressure to stir my cock. "What's your name, stranger?"

I could easily be the Jack to her Jane, but I want to hear my name from those lips tonight. "Evan."

The look on her face is all surprise and awe like I've already got two fingers inside her and I'm honed in on that spot that will etch my name into her memory forever. "Is that your real name?"

I crane my neck to look at the lobby. The last thing I need right now is for anyone I work with to breeze past us and call me *Dr. Scott.* I have to get this woman into a hotel room and out of that dress now.

"According to my driver's license, it is." I circle the pad of my thumb on her palm before I let her hand go. "I'm going inside to refill my drink and then I'm heading upstairs. Can I get you anything, Jane?"

She reaches up to touch her neck. It's a subtle sign that she wants my hand, or maybe my mouth, there. "Are you inviting me up to your room?"

Technically, I'm inviting her to a room I haven't rented yet. I was out here catching a breath of frigid nor'easter air. I did my time inside when I took the podium, ran through an off-the-cuff speech about the boatload of accolades my boss acquired in his career and then handed him a silver wristwatch courtesy of his wife. He threw the goddamn shindig on his own dime and then expected me to kiss ass in public to hold onto a job I'm not sure I want.

"If you are, I'm game," Jane tosses that jewel out before I have a chance to offer a formal invitation to get naked with me. "I didn't notice you at the ceremony. Are you a friend of the bride or the groom?"

It's the obvious conclusion to jump to. I'm dressed in a tuxedo. There's a wedding reception in the ballroom tonight. She has no clue that I was just in the hotel's five-star restaurant with a group that consists of primarily sixty-something-year-old surgeons all desperate to one-up each other with elaborate descriptions of their summer homes.

At thirty-four I'm the baby of the bunch, hence the reason I'm standing in the bitter cold with a drink in my hand contemplating why I went to medical school in the first place.

Jane marches on, nerves twitching at the edge of her words. "I'm a friend of Leanna. I'm actually one of her bridesmaids. I had to get the hell out of there when Henry started talking about how committed he is to her. It's bullshit. You know that, don't you? He totally screwed her over this past summer when he was in Vegas. She forgave him and now they're married. Can you believe that?"

"Henry is a selfish son-of-a-bitch."

Her eyes flick up to meet mine. "What's your room number?"

The snow starts again, large flakes of unwanted inconvenience. I need a condom. My gaze darts up and down the street. Other than a restaurant a block over, every other storefront and business are locked up tight.

Late Sunday night will do that to Manhattan. A snowstorm doesn't help.

"You have protection, right?" Pretty Jane reads my mind like a sensual sorceress. "I didn't bring any condoms with me."

Normally, I'd have at least a few tucked in my pocket, but I got dressed at the hospital. An emergency surgery this afternoon cut into my prep time for this hellish evening, so I had my rental tux delivered. I changed in the locker room and forgot one of the essentials. The breath mints made it into my pants pocket next to my wallet, but the condoms didn't.

Fucking great.

I'm not sending this woman on a mission to get me a rubber. That comes with the risk of her bailing on me because she doesn't see the effort as worth the reward.

It's worth it, in spades, or in her case, orgasms.

"I've got that covered, or should I say, it will be covered," I quip with a tip of my glass before I down the last swallow. I'll go floor-by-floor and door-to-door in this hotel to find a condom if need be. "Do you need to say goodbye to Leanna before you bail?"

She blows an adorable puff of air out from between her lips. "I do. I left my purse in there. What about you?"

"I didn't have a purse that matched my outfit tonight," I joke. "I'll meet you in the lobby in thirty minutes. We can head up to the room together."

"Make it fifteen," she counters, a challenge woven into her tone. "I'll take a Bellini."

"Consider it done," I whisper as she breezes past me, the maimed umbrella dragging behind her.

The doorman jumps into action and props open the heavy glass door. Jane steps into the vestibule just as the ugly winter wind gives not only me but the doorman, the early holiday gift of an eyeful of her luscious ass.

Something tells me this night is going to be one for the record books.

Chapter 2

Evan

"Your money is no good here, sir." The obviously exasperated hotel desk clerk pushes my credit card back at me. "I told you twice already that we are booked solid for the night."

Well, shit.

On any other night, I would have tipped my hat to fate and given up. The reason for that is simple. In my world, there's never been a shortage of no-strings attached fun. If I don't get my recommended daily allowance today, I'll make up for it tomorrow, or whenever my brutal schedule allows me the good fortune of enough time for a screw.

I'm not a minute man. I take my time. I savor every second I'm with a beautiful woman because sex is my salvation. It's what keeps me sane in a world where I hold the keys to the kingdoms that are other people's futures.

Tonight I'm off the clock and tomorrow is an all-too-rare day off for me, so I'm partying like it's my birthday since I spent most of that in surgery. I fought like a warrior to save the life of a man twice my age.

He got his second chance. There's not a better birthday gift in the world than that.

"We have another location in the East Village. I can inquire if there is a room available there for you." The desk clerk types something into the keyboard of the computer in front of him.

I'm tempted to ask him how the hell he thinks I'll get there since the storm has forced the city to shut down but I refrain from flying my asshole flag tonight. There's always a work around when my cock is on a mission.

"Thanks, but I'll figure something out." I scoop up the money that I thought would be substantial enough to bribe him into giving me a room.

I've checked into enough hotels to know how it works. It's not uncommon for the staff to hold one room for the guy who shows up in the middle of the night. Generally, he's so desperate for a place to lay his head that he'll pay whatever the hell the ransom is.

It looks like some schmuck beat me to the finish line tonight.

"Evan, I thought you took off an hour ago."

I smile inwardly at the sound of Dr. Jordan Whitman's voice as it carries through the lobby. Jordan's got a room key in his pocket and since the party has an open bar, he won't be going anywhere until the last drop of free alcohol has slid down his throat.

"I need to borrow your room." I slap him on the back. "You owe me for handling that carotid stenting on Mr. Brilton last month."

"I repaid that when I took on Judith Lancaster as a patient two weeks ago. She requested you and I agreed to see her to even our score. There's nothing wrong with her and she calls me every day at ten a.m. sharp." His blond brows pinch together. "What do you need my room for?"

Jordan is a leader in the field of cardiology but he's the only thirty-eight-year-old guy I know who is lugging around a permanent set of blue balls.

It started and ended his senior year of high school when he made his move on a cheerleader. He got head and then a quickie in the back seat of his car. That one and only encounter is the only action his dick has ever seen. It's not a surprise that he isn't putting two and two together.

"I met a woman." I pull him into a half-assed man hug. Our shoulders bump. "The hotel is booked up solid and I need a room to entertain her in."

"Entertain her?" His gaze narrows. "I don't get it."

At any other time, I'd jump on the chance to throw his pseudo virginity back in his face. I can't tonight. Time is running out and I need a room stat.

"I'm going to screw her, Jordan." I lower my voice. "I need a room and a condom and if you help me out with the room, I'll owe you twice over. I'll take over the Lancaster file."

He scratches the outer shell of his ear. "You need a condom? I've got one."

Why?

I don't ask the question even though I want to. I was prepared to go back into the restaurant to beg the bartender for a condom. The dude has serious game. There's no doubt in my mind he's got a half dozen condoms tucked in his back pocket. "Give me the room key and the condom."

His mouth twists wryly. "Deal but I have two conditions."

I'm so eager to get Jane Smith out of that frilly dress that I'll give Jordan my left nut at this point. I don't need it. The right one is that impressive.

"What do you want?" I ask even though I don't give a shit what it is.

"It's a two bedroom suite so don't use the main bedroom. I'm not sleeping in a bed you had sex on."

"A two bedroom suite?" I have to ask. "Why do you need a two bedroom suite?"

He stares at me for a minute, his arms crossed over his chest. "I booked a room here because I invited my mom to Manhattan for the party and my apartment isn't big enough for the two of us. I wanted her to meet the people I work with. Her flight was canceled because of the storm."

I have compassion. I get where he's coming from. My parents are both doctors so impressing either of them is an impossible task. I gave up trying right around my twelfth birthday.

"Fine. I'll do it in the other room." I look at my watch. "What's the other condition?"

"Get Kylie to agree to have dinner with me."

That's like asking the iceberg to politely get the hell out of the way of the Titanic. Dr. Kylie Newman won't budge on her stance to never date Jordan.

I've been called a miracle worker in the past, so I won't say never when it comes to Kylie and Dr. Blue Balls.

"You've got yourself a deal." I hold out my hand waiting for my two tickets to a few unforgettable hours with Jane Smith. "I'll text you when I'm done with the room."

***

"Do you do this often?" Jane's gaze roams my face as the elevator creeps its way up to the twenty-third floor.

I half-expected her to bail on me after I'd pocketed Jordan's room key and his one and only condom. I've had sex with enough strangers to know that second thoughts are the number one enemy of potential one-night stands.

Sometimes a woman thinks it's a good idea to hook up with a stranger until she has a minute to sit on that decision or she's phoned a friend from the ladies' room.

It's no harm, no foul to me.

I want to be a fond memory to the women I fuck, not a regret.

"Not as often as you think," I answer truthfully. My schedule is to blame for that. The few short-term relationships I've had the last few years are a contributing factor too. "What about you?"

"Does it matter?"

Hell, no. Her sexual history is about as important to me in this moment as her favorite color. She's a willing adult. That's all I need to know.

"The only thing that matters to me tonight is that we both have a good time."

She lets out a long exhale. "I need a good time."

I take a step forward as the elevator dings our arrival on the twenty-third floor. I turn to look at her once the doors fly open. "After you, Jane."

It's obvious from the sly smile on her face that she understands the double meaning of my words.

I'll give her what she needs before I take what I want.

It's always ladies first in my world and Jane is about to find that out.

Chapter 3

Chloe

Jane Smith?

As soon as I said the name, I knew it was a mistake.

I always imagined if I had a one-night stand that I'd use an exotic fake name, not a common name that virtually every woman who has slept with a stranger has used.

I watch Evan as he unlocks the hotel room door with the key card in his hand.

He is, without a doubt, the best looking man I've met in a very long time. I didn't notice him at the wedding before we ran into each other outside. That doesn't surprise me since there are hundreds of people in the ballroom of this hotel, all celebrating a marriage that likely won't last a year.

The glass in my hand shakes as I follow Evan into his hotel room.

I don't drink often. When I do, it's usually a half of a glass of white wine with dinner, but tonight I thought I'd need courage to follow through with my decision to go to a hotel room with a stranger. I haven't taken a sip of the Bellini, and I doubt I will. My stomach has been doing flip-flops ever since I agreed to come up to his room.

I almost hit the emergency button in the elevator to stop this entire thing in its tracks. I want this, but the nagging voice in the back of my mind is telling me that I'm going to regret it. I'm telling it to shut up and so far, I'm winning.

On our way up I asked him whether he does this often without thinking through the possibility that he'd ask me the very same thing. I didn't want to tell him that I've never had a one-night stand, so instead, I asked him if it mattered if I did.

Coming across as a bitch wasn't part of my plan.

Unfortunately, it sometimes happens when I'm nervous as hell.

"Are you from New York?" I ask that to close the gap of uncomfortable silence that sits between us. I have no idea if making small talk is expected when you're on the cusp of crawling into bed with a complete stranger.

He drops the key card on a desk that's just inside the door of the suite. It's much more impressive than the room I was in earlier. Leanna ordered the other five bridesmaids and me to her hotel room late this afternoon to help her get ready.

It was cramped, but no one cared. We spent the time leading up to the ceremony sharing stories about the bride while she had her hair and makeup done.

When it was my turn I talked about our law school days. It wasn't overly sentimental because that's not who Leanna is. She didn't shed one tear at all today on what is supposed to be the happiest day of her life. She knows exactly who her new husband is and what he did in Las Vegas. The only positive is that there were three divorce attorneys in attendance.

I have a feeling at least one of them will be taking her on as a new client before the end of next year.

"I grew up in California, but I live here now," he offers as he loosens his black necktie. "What about you?"

My life started in Pennsylvania and then my journey dotted the landscape of the country before I ended up in New York City days before my tenth birthday. He doesn't want to know all of that, so I keep the answer short and sweet. "I've lived here long enough that I consider myself a New Yorker."

That draws a smile to his lips. "Who called you a coward, Jane?"

I thought the promise of no-strings-attached sex would wipe that memory from his mind, but it hasn't. I had no idea he was standing in the shadows when I walked out into the bitter cold. I needed to catch my breath after an infuriating discussion I had with Gretchen, one of the other bridesmaids.

She called me a coward when I scoffed at her suggestion that I have dinner with her brother. I hate blind dates. I've never been on one that has ended with the anticipation of a second date.

Gretchen made a point of telling me that she doesn't believe I'm adventurous enough. It stung because she's right. I can count on one hand the times I've done anything spur-of-the-moment or out-of-the-ordinary. Four of those were before my eighteenth birthday eleven years ago.

"No one important," I answer as I set my glass down on the coffee table. "For the record, I'm not a coward."

"You came up to a hotel room with a man you just met. If that's not brave, I don't know what is."

I know what is, but that's not a conversation I have with just anyone, especially a man I'll never see again after tonight.

I feel a pang of something when I think about that. I like him, and it's not just because his eyes are mesmerizing and his smile is genuine. I can sense that he's considerate even though the only thing he's done for me so far is buy me a drink.

If only a guy like this was waiting for me when I agreed to a blind date. I can already tell that we'd talk for hours. He's approachable and patient. He's also hot-as-sin. His brown hair is just the right length for me to fist in my hands.

"I want to kiss you, Jane." He slides his jacket from his shoulders, taking care to drape it over the back of a blue armchair. "I've wanted to kiss you since you turned around when we were outside."

I don't care if the words are honest or not. I've wanted to kiss him since then too. My body speaks for me as I take a step closer to him.

He closes the remaining distance in an instant and then his full, soft lips crash down on mine and I know that I'm never going to forget this night or this man.

Chapter 4

Evan

I stripped her slowly after we kissed.

That kiss made me weak in the knees. The last time that happened I was in grade school and Mary Bowman planted a wet one on my cheek during recess. We agreed to go steady, but our inability to communicate because of my shyness ended my first budding relationship within the week.

Thankfully, I've come out of my shell since then. If I hadn't, I sure as hell wouldn't be in the position I am right now.

I'm still dressed, but beautiful Jane is not thanks to me.

She's sprawled on her back on the bed; her blonde hair fanned around her head. She looks like every dream I've ever had since I first experienced the insane pleasure of being with a woman.

Small waist, supple breasts, and soft curves.

I rest a knee on the bed and lean down to kiss her again. It's a dangerous move because my dick is as hard as steel in my pants. It's straining against the zipper of this rental tux. Another taste of her mouth will inch me closer to coming.

She moans into the kiss this time as her hand circles the back of my neck. Her touch is soft and tender. She's not trying to control anything. I can tell that she wants me to set the pace.

I break the kiss and trace a slow path with my lips down her neck. Her skin is sweet. It's peppered with a light coat of some fragrant lotion. Beneath that is the scent of her. It's intoxicating and arousing.

I can't remember a time when I've wanted a woman this much.

"Evan." My name escapes her lips as I hone in on the smooth skin of her stomach.

I'm grateful as fuck that I told her my real name when we met. I've never heard it laced with this much desire and need before.

I glide my lips along her hip before I kiss a small mole on her outer thigh.

Her breathing quickens. It's an audible leap from measured and deep to rapid and shallow. Her legs twitch as she tries to hide her arousal. I know she's wet. I felt it when I slid her lace panties down her legs.

I glide a finger along the seam of her pussy and it brings a sound to her lips. It's not a moan, but a sigh. It's soft, barely noticeable but I hear it.

I'm acutely aware of everything right now as if my senses have all been turned up so each sound, smell, and taste will become etched into my memory.

Taste.

I crave it so much that I don't waste another second. I lower my mouth to her pussy, inching the tip of my tongue over her swollen clit before I dip it inside.

She's exquisite. I lap at her, gentle lashes of my tongue against her clit before I suck it between my teeth.

Her hips move as her hands find my hair.

I swear to fuck that makes me even harder. Her fingers are eager and restless as she tugs me closer. She wants this as much as I do. Her need to get off is controlling it all; her movements, those fucking sweet sounds she's making and the wetness.

With each stroke of my tongue against her, she gets wetter and wetter and for the first time in my life, I wish to fuck I could slide my dick in completely bare so I could experience the slickness of skin touching skin.

"Evan," she murmurs and I thrust my groin into the bed. I'm primed to fuck. I need it. I feel like a caged animal, but I won't take until she's given me what I want.

I need to watch her come apart. I'm craving it more than the intense rush I already know I'm going to feel when her pussy envelops my cock.

"Give it to me…"I stop myself before I say *Jane* because that's not her goddamn name. I'd trade everything I own at this moment just to know it. "Come on my face."

She grinds herself against my mouth.

It's so fucking hot that I moan into her flesh and that's enough to push her over.

She comes and it's the most beautiful thing I've ever seen. Her body pulsates, her lips part and she says my name, my real fucking name, draped in a moan.

***

My hands shake as I wrap my dick in the condom Jordan gave me. I'm not nervous about the fuck. I want this. After what I just witnessed, all I need in life to die a happy man is to be inside of this woman.

I watch her as she takes in the sight of me stroking my cock. She hasn't made a sound since she came. She also hasn't moved beyond craning her neck so she could watch as I rid myself of all of my clothes before I tore open the condom package.

I can't shake the desire to stop time. I'm going to fuck her, we'll both get off and then we'll dress and part ways.

The thought of that is invading everything. I already want more of her and I've yet to shoot my load.

"Evan?" she whispers my name.

I jerk my chin up. "Yes?"

"Your mouth is amazing."

Her words shred the small amount of self-control I have left. I've been prolonging this because I don't want it to be over. I could stare at her for hours like this with her skin flushed from her release and her fingers lightly strumming her clit.

I crawl onto the bed and move until I'm above her, my hands bracketing either side of her head. I look down and into those stormy hazel eyes. "You're a beautiful woman."

Her gaze trails over my face slowly. I don't need her to return the compliment. I know she likes what she sees.

The pulsing need in my cock takes over and I inch closer to her wetness. As her eyelids flutter shut, I push in and the groan that escapes me comes from somewhere so deep inside that I don't recognize it.

I take it slowly at first, letting her tight body adapt to me.

She moans loudly when I speed up the pace. "Yes, Evan, yes."

I dip my head to hide the smile as I brush my mouth over her left nipple. I take it between my teeth as I pound into her over and over knowing that this fuck is going to stay with me long after tonight.

I grunt with each rock of my hips and when her fingernails carve a path down my back to my ass, my balls tighten.

I fuck her hard until her sex clenches around my throbbing dick with her orgasm and then I empty my load with a jackhammering in my heart that I've never felt before.

Chapter 5

Chloe

I tug my dress back over my head while he's in the washroom. He didn't say anything after we both came. He held me briefly and then stood up. I'm not sure what I was expecting since this is the only one-night stand I've ever had.

Am I supposed to leave before he reappears?

Do I wait around so I can thank him for what just happened?

I'm tempted to text my friend, Gabi, to ask. I wouldn't call her an expert on one-night stand protocol but I know she's had at least two so in our small world, she has more experience than I do.

"Can I see you again?"

His wickedly sexy voice pulls me from my thoughts. I turn toward it, wanting to get at least one more parting glance of his face.

I'm gifted with much more than that. He's nude. His spectacular body is on full display and framed by the light filtering in from the washroom.

He's sculpted and muscular; the definition of perfection. He must spend half of his time at the gym. If I looked as good as he does, I'd stand naked in front of a stranger too.

"Jane?" He huffs out a laugh with a shake of his head. "Give me your real name and tell me when I can see you again."

"How do you know that my real name isn't Jane?"

"I know." He steps closer to where I'm standing next to the bed. "You used that name because you didn't want to know me. You do now."

"Do I?" I try to laugh too but it comes out more like a desperate cackle.

"You enjoyed yourself tonight."

I don't know why but I like that he's confident enough to make declarations about what I'm feeling. He's right but I don't want him to know that.

"You enjoyed yourself too, Evan."

"You're fucking right I did." He bends to pick up his boxer briefs. "I want to enjoy myself again so tell me when that will happen."

This may be my first one-night stand but I know that by definition they last one single night and then the connection is over, forever. I don't need any complications in my life at this point. I'm still trying to untangle myself from the only relationship I've ever had with a man.

"I think we should walk out of this room as strangers who shared a good time. "

"I've had my tongue inside of you." He cocks a dark brow. "We're not strangers anymore."

A little burst of laughter escapes me before I bite my bottom lip. "I guess I can't argue that point, can I?"

I watch as he finishes dressing, taking note of the fact that he tugs his phone from the front pocket of his pants.

"Give me your real name and number." His gravelly voice travels right to my core.

I don't think I'll ever forget the sound of it or any other part of him. A man like this doesn't cross my path often...well, never, if I'm being truthful.

"I don't think that's a good idea," I say reluctantly.

I know that he's looking for another hook up and if I thought I could handle that, I'd take his phone from his hand and key my contact information in myself. He's the kind of man I could get addicted to. Eventually, I'd want more and that can't happen.

"Why not?" He eyes me. "We're sexually compatible. We like each other."

"You like me," I shoot back. "I didn't say I like you."

The corners of his full mouth rise into a brilliant smile revealing perfectly straight white teeth. "You like me, Jane. You want to see me again."

"I'm not giving you my name or number."

"Fair enough." He steps even closer. "I won't push but let me make something clear."

I swallow hard as I look up at him. "What?"

"I'm going to spend weeks, if not months, stopping every blonde I see on the streets of Manhattan in the hope that it's you."

I want to say that I doubt he'll remember me after tonight, but the intense look on his face tells me that there's at least a seed of truth in his words.

He's sinfully handsome. He wants me and all my insecurities are screaming that I need to walk out of this room and away from him forever.

He starts toward the main room and I follow, knowing that the chances that we'll run into each other again are slim. New York City isn't a big place but it's filled with millions of faces and over time it's easy to forget someone you spent only a few hours with.

"I'll call down to the front desk to have them flag down a taxi for you, Jane."

It's considerate. It's also unnecessary. There are a fleet of cars with drivers at the ready for anyone attending the wedding that needs a ride home tonight. The reception isn't set to end for another thirty minutes so I'll be able to get back to my apartment without a problem. "I have that covered."

He leans down and brushes his lips over mine. "Get home safely, beautiful. I promise I won't follow you."

A smile teases the corner of my mouth. I should walk out of here and not look back. We had fun and if we part like this, I'll have the memory of this night forever.

I reach for the door handle and then turn back to get one last look at him. His hair is mussed, his shirt is dishevelled and he's eyeing me with a need that is palpable. I could leave and try my best to forget about him, or I can guarantee that our paths cross again.

I look him straight in the eye. "If you happen to stop by the Roasting Point Café at the corner of Lexington and 42nd any weekday morning around eight, you'll find that blonde you're looking for."

"Good to know, Jane. That's good to know," he says with a sly grin before I turn and leave, with the hope that I'll see him bright and early on Monday morning.

Chapter 6

Chloe

I stand near the glass door and sip my tea
while I scan the face of every man who enters the
café. I know that I'll recognize Evan as soon as I see
him even if I have no idea if he'll be wearing a suit
and tie, jeans or gym clothes.

This is the third morning that I've stood in this
spot waiting until eight fifteen before I head out the
door and walk two blocks to my office.

When he didn't show on Monday, I convinced
myself it was because he didn't want to appear too
eager. Yesterday, I decided that reason he wasn't in
the café was related to a busy schedule. It's
Wednesday now, and I'm running out of excuses for
why he's not here.

That's not entirely true. I do have an idea
about why he hasn't walked through the entrance.
Saturday night was fun, but maybe when dawn broke
on Sunday morning, he realized that our one-night
stand needed to remain a memory from his past and
not become part of his future.

I look down at the screen of my phone. It's
now seventeen minutes past eight, and I have a client
meeting me at my office in thirteen minutes. If I leave
now, I'll make it with little time to spare.

I start toward the door trying to subtly push
my way past the people walking into the café. Ever
since this place opened a year-and-a-half ago, it's
been steadily becoming more popular.

There was a time when I could walk in and have my tea in my hand within three minutes. Now, I'm lucky if I get in and out in twenty.

"Hey." A hand brushes against my shoulder. "What are the chances that I'd see you here?"

I'd know that voice with my eyes closed. It's deep and comforting. I turn toward the man who is now standing beside me. "I'd say you had at least a ninety percent chance of seeing me here since you do almost every Wednesday morning."

He leans down to kiss me square on the forehead. "Those are good odds."

"Spoken like a true poker champion." I reach forward to adjust the dark scarf around his neck. "Did you walk all the way here from your place?"

My stepbrother, Rocco Jones, gives me a curt nod. "It's ten blocks. If I can't walk that far in sub-zero weather, I shouldn't be living in this city."

I study his ruggedly handsome face. The tip of his nose is red, his blue eyes are watering and his dark brown hair is pushed back from his forehead. "What's her name, Rocco?"

"Who?" He cups his hands together in front of his mouth and blows on them. "What are you talking about?"

"You haven't shaved in days. That's usually because you've been holed up somewhere with a woman. So, who is she?"

"This is insulation from the cold." He rubs his hand over the light beard that is covering his jaw. "I have a meeting this afternoon, so it'll be history before noon."

Rocco's life couldn't be any more different than mine. He made a small fortune playing professional poker before he invested in a game app that blew up worldwide. Now, he spends his time funding the business ideas of others.

My days are devoted to employment law.

"I have to get to my office." I reach up to give him a quick hug. "I'm going to Pop's for dinner tonight. Can I count on you coming? Nash and Luke will be there."

"The infamous Jones family dinner, " he drawls. "When's the last time we all had dinner with Pop? You know how emotional he is when all four of his kids are sitting around the dining room table."

I know how emotional he is. I know how I am too when I hear any of my three stepbrothers refer to me as their sibling. Even though my surname is still legally Newell, I'm a Jones in every way that counts.

"I'll take that as a yes." I glance back at the entrance, but there's still no sign of Evan. "I'm going to work. I'll see you tonight."

"Who is he?"

"Who?" I try to keep my tone light. Rocco is the eldest of my brothers and he's always been the most protective of me.

"The guy you keep looking for." He stares past my shoulder at the entrance.

"No one, " I say with a sigh. "I'm not looking for a guy."

It's not a lie. I'm done waiting with baited breath for Evan to show up. I got my hopes up that I'd see him again but I need to resign myself to the reality that we had one night together and that's where our story ends.

Chapter 7

Evan

I look up at the clock that's hanging on the wall in the recovery room. Five minutes after ten. *Fuck. Just Fuck.*

Today is the third in a row I've missed meeting *Jane* at the café. I was in a scheduled surgery on Monday morning at eight a.m., and yesterday it was a consultation with a former patient that kept me from seeing the woman I can't stop thinking about.

I was done my rounds at seven this morning and had every intention of breaking free of this place to head uptown. Those plans were sidelined by the repair of a torn artery in the leg of a woman who had been hit by a car.

The patient is going to be fine after extensive recovery.

Unless I can manage to get my ass to the Roasting Point Café tomorrow morning, I'm not going to be fine. I want to see the mysterious blonde. I'm craving another kiss and I've been aching for a chance to fuck her again.

"Did you talk to Kylie about me?" Jordan approaches from the left.

I scrub my hand over my forehead. "I'm good, Jordan. Thanks for asking."

He laughs. "I'll take that as a no. I held up my end of the agreement. You need to follow through on your end."

His end of our agreement consisted of him chatting up the wife of our boss while he filled up on free vodka. My end is a hell of a lot more complicated.

Kylie Newman is a retired model turned vascular surgeon. She's got at least ten years experience on me and the last guy she dated was a rock star on Wall Street.

She's out of Jordan's league but I always honor my word, so I'll pitch the idea of a lunch date with Jordan to her and let fate take hold of the wheel.

"I'll talk to Kylie this afternoon." I nod to the nurse who is waiting to speak to me. "I've got another surgery in an hour and then three consultations. Is your dance card full too?"

He shakes his head as he eyes up the blonde nurse.

She's cute and married. Vanessa Ryan is one of the superstars in this ward. I rely on her heavily to keep me updated on the progress of my patients. "She's married, Jordan, and our co-worker."

"It doesn't hurt to look," he quips. "Why are all the hot ones taken?"

"Just a guess, but it might be because they found men who don't stare at them like a fucking creep."

"You're an asshole," he volleys back with a wide grin.

I toss Vanessa a smile before I turn to walk toward her. "You're right, but it works for me."

***

I powered through my day, fully focused in surgery and wholly invested in every consultation. I even convinced Kylie to have lunch in the hospital cafeteria with Jordan next week. I agreed to be the third wheel, but Jordan won't know that until he finds me sitting next to him chowing down on an underdressed egg salad sandwich. I'd rate the day a success except that I can't shake thoughts of Jane from my mind.

"I wanted to thank you again for the tickets to the Islanders game, Evan." Vanessa stops making notes on the chart in her hands to look up at me. "Garrett is over the moon. Date nights have been few and far between lately. We both appreciate it."

Garrett Ryan, Vanessa's husband, is one of the good guys. We met on Vanessa's birthday when he stopped in to drop off a bouquet of flowers and a birthday cake so the staff could celebrate with her.

We hit it off. I've been invited to their home twice for dinner since that day and both times an emergency nixed the plans. I'm still waiting on another offer, but I know they devote the bulk of their time at home to their daughter, Ruthie.

"It's my pleasure," I say, looking at her. "A friend has season tickets, but he couldn't use them. I know how much you two love hockey."

She wrinkles her nose. "Garrett loves hockey. I love Garrett, so it's perfect."

I feel the phone in my pocket vibrate. I already know who it is. Jack Pearce. We're supposed to meet for dinner, but he's grown accustomed to me being a no-show. I couldn't ask for a better friend. He'd say the same about me.

"Are you going to get that?" Vanessa cocks her head. "You're off the clock. You should get out of here and have a life while you can."

"It's just a friend. He can entertain himself until I decide if I'm meeting him for a burger or not."

"If I had a vote, I'd say meet him for a burger." She shrugs. "You've been working non-stop. You deserve a night off. Besides, you never know who might be in the restaurant. My friend, Bridget, met her husband at a restaurant. They were both having dinner with other people and then, bam, they saw each other and everything changed."

I pinch the bridge of my nose. "I think I have a better chance of having a bam moment inside the Roasting Point on Lexington at the crack of dawn than a burger place in midtown tonight."

"That's oddly specific." She laughs. "Should I ask what that's about?"

"Ask me tomorrow morning after eight. With any luck, I'll have had my bam moment and I'll know the name of the woman I can't stop thinking about."

Chapter 8

Chloe

"You were quiet during dinner, Chloe."

I look to where my stepdad is standing next to the dining room table. He'd cooked a feast for my brothers and me. I smelled his signature chicken potpie as soon as I let myself into his house in Queens.

He gave all four of us a key the day he moved into the small house. That was almost a year ago. I can tell that he's still not as comfortable here as he was back in the apartment in Manhattan he shared with my mom, but he's finding his way.

"I'm tired, dad." I swipe a towel over a plate before I place it back in the cupboard above the sink. "I've been at the office late almost every night for weeks."

He picks up the last of the dirty dishes and carries them to where I'm standing. "You might have a case of the winter blues."

I know his tried and true remedy for that. "I've got a full caseload right now, so California is out of the question."

He huffs out a low laugh. "You read my mind. Do you remember how we used to head there for a week right after Christmas?"

I remember everything about those trips. We'd take off the day after Christmas. My three brothers would sit in one row of seats on the airplane, while I sat between my parents in the row behind them.

It was our only family vacation each year. We made the most of those seven days and as soon as we landed back in New York, we'd start counting the days until the next one.

The trips were a family tradition until I started college and my folks traded the sunny beaches of California for Florida's gulf coast and a week with their friends who had retired there.

"How could I forget?" I kiss his cheek. He's still as handsome as the day I met him. He sports a few more wrinkles now and his brown hair is an appealing mix of salt and pepper. The big difference that I see when I look at him now is sadness in his eyes that wasn't there before. "Maybe next December we can go back?"

Tipping his chin up, he looks at the open cupboard, his eyes not focusing on anything in particular. I know he's lost in thought. "I'll start planning it next month."

He will. He lives for the moments that he spends with my brothers and I. We've all encouraged him to get out and meet new people, but he always says that he knows everyone he needs to. I don't push because if he's content in the small world he lives in, I'm content too.

"You barely spoke to your brothers during dinner," he says quietly. "Granted, it's hard to get a word in when those three are around, but still, you're not yourself."

He's right. I'm not. I listened to my brother, Luke, share the details about a fire he responded to last week. He loves working as a fireman and every time I see him, he has another tale of heroism to share. Those stories are never about him, although he has risked his life on numerous occasions to help others.

Nash is just as talkative. Today, he went on about a campaign he landed. He started his own advertising business seven years ago when he was twenty-five and it's steadily growing. He's the middle son, but the soft gray at his temples makes him look older than Rocco, even though he's two years younger.

I clutch the towel in my fist as I make a small confession. "I met someone, dad. I like him, but…"

"But, what?" His gaze narrows, his brown eyes rich with concern.

I can't exactly tell my father that I hooked up with a random at my friend's wedding. My dad is strictly old school. He practically went on my first date with me.

His recollection of that night is different than mine, but I distinctly remember him being in the movie theatre while I sat next to my date eating popcorn. I may have only been fourteen, but having your dad tag along to watch every move of the boy you like is a sure way to end the date early.

"What did this man do, Chloe? Tell me."

"He didn't do anything." I twist the towel in my hands. "I thought I'd see him again. That hasn't happened yet. We hit it off, but maybe I felt a spark that he didn't."

"That's impossible," he blurts out. "You're everything any man could ever want."

Spoken like a father who loves his only daughter.

"It doesn't matter either way." I busy myself with washing another plate. "I like my life the way it is. I don't need a man."

His hand dives into the warm sudsy water to cover mine. "We all need someone who cares for us. If he's not that guy, you'll find him. I promise you that the man you're meant to spend your life with is out there looking for you right now."

That might be true, but the man I'd like to spend at least a few more hours with knows exactly where to find me every morning at eight sharp. That man is obviously not looking for me.

Chapter 9

Evan

I was tempted to turn off my phone when I finally got into bed well past midnight. Yesterday was a bitch, and even though I wasn't on call overnight, I fell asleep with the fear that I'd end up back at the hospital before dawn broke.

That didn't happen.

I got a few hours of much-needed sleep, shaved and took a shower. Then I dressed in jeans, a gray sweater and my black wool coat. I left my apartment in plenty of time to get to the Roasting Point on Lexington by eight.

It's now eight-fifteen and Jane is nowhere to be found.

It's Thursday. That means I missed my chance on three consecutive mornings. For all I know she gave up and is hitting up another café for an espresso or whatever gets her motor running.

The other possibility is that sweet Jane lied through her teeth about frequenting this place, but my now-hardening cock is telling me otherwise.

That's because a gorgeous blonde just walked in. The blonde I've been aching to see for days.

Her hair is pulled up into a high ponytail. She's wearing a dark trench coat and carrying a leather briefcase.

She looks like a high-powered executive.

Jane is even hotter this morning than she was the night we met.

I rub the back of my neck as I feel my pulse race. I'm not like this around women. I've never been, yet I feel my heartbeat speed as I study her from across the café. I should be up on my feet by now, stalking toward her.

In my mind's eye, I've already got her in an embrace and I'm dipping her and kissing her like I wanted to before she walked out of Jordan's hotel room the other night.

I sit with that image for a second as Jane finally scans the entire space before her gaze locks with mine.

***

"Jane," I say as I approach her, irritated that I'm not greeting her with the name everyone in her world knows.

"You're here." Her eyes widen as I stop in front of where she's standing. "I didn't think I'd see you again, Evan."

I move a half step to lean in for a kiss but stop myself. We fucked in a hotel room. We're not long lost friends who engage in double cheek kisses when we see each other.

My gaze goes back to her face. I was riding a slight buzz from the bourbon the other night. I knew she was attractive, but not this striking. This woman is beautiful, as in, breathtaking.

"You told me you'd be here," I go on quickly. "I would have been here earlier in the week, but work has been hell."

She nods like she half believes me. It's not bullshit and if I confess that I spend most of my time caring for others there would most likely be immediate understanding in her eyes.

Most women react the same way when I tell them what I do for a living. They're impressed. Visions of me in a white coat with a stethoscope around my neck, and a luxury apartment bordering Central Park dance in their heads.

The reality is that I spend the bulk of my time in scrubs as a means to pay off the debt I incurred while studying to be a surgeon. Expertise isn't cheap and my apartment speaks to that. It's a bare-bones bachelor in Morningside Heights.

It's a place for me to crash when I can. It's all I need right now. That and five more minutes with Jane.

"What's your real name?" I ask as she opens her pouty pink lips to respond to my comment about my absence from the café every morning this week.

Her mouth slams shut. She looks around before her gaze levels back on my face. "I told you my name is Jane Smith."

I step closer to her as a guy slips past me on his way to the counter where three baristas are standing at the ready to prepare his overpriced water-downed, coffee. "Bullshit. Jane isn't your real name."

The corners of her lips jerk up into a smile before she thins them. "You don't know that. You might be surprised to learn that there are women in this city who are named Jane Smith."

"I've met some, many…most," I stop myself before I

confess my number to her. Hell, I don't know it. Ballpark might be fifty… a year, multiplied by…

"Good for you," Jane interrupts my less-than-stellar mental math skills. "I have to get to work. I'm running late today."

"Have dinner with me," I blurt that out as if I'm a regular nine-to-fiver who controls his life and schedule. "I'd like to see you again."

She looks at me, her gaze scanning my face. "When do you want to have dinner?"

Tonight, but I know that's not possible. I'm scheduled for surgery at three this afternoon. My dinner is going to consist of a candy bar I purchase from the vending machine once my patient is alert and awake in recovery.

"If you give me your number, I can call you when I know I have a free night."

She looks to where my phone is peeking out of the top of my coat pocket. "How many Jane Smiths are listed in your contacts?"

Four; they're referenced by hair color and eye color.

"The other night was a lot of fun," Jane goes on before I can get a word in. "I'm not looking for anything serious right now, and you're obviously a very busy man."

I'm a fucking doctor who sold his soul for a lousy paycheck and the chance to save lives. It's worth it for the most part, until you want more.

I want more now.

"What are you doing at noon today?" I pat my phone. "I don't need your number, Jane. Meet me for an hour so we can get to know each other better. We'll start with your real name."

She tilts her head as her gaze narrows. "You want to meet me for an hour today? For lunch or something else? You didn't say anything about food."

I raise an eyebrow. I'm all for skipping food for a good fuck. I can't read this woman so

I clarify because my cock is swelling and the sudden rush of blood to it is cutting off any chance I have for rational and clear thought. "Are you going to be hungry at noon, Jane?"

She shakes her head from side-to-side, her hazel eyes meeting mine. "I ate a big breakfast."

Why the fuck is that turning me on?

I throw caution to the wind because I want this woman. Fuck do I want her. "There's a Bishop Hotel on the corner. We can meet there if you think that'll work for you."

"That works for me," she says as she shifts her briefcase from one hand to the other. "I'll meet you in the lobby at noon, Evan."

I have to wait for three-and-a-half hours to touch her. This is going to be the longest morning of my life.

Chapter 10

Chloe

Since when do I agree to meet men for *nooners?* I think that's the appropriate term to use when you arrange an hour-long meeting in a hotel in the middle of the day.

I have no idea what came over me back at the café when I saw Evan. My first response was disbelief. That was washed away almost immediately with a wave of excitement.

When he proposed the idea that we meet at noon, I assumed it was for sex. My desire to be with him again is to blame for that. I don't know if he was planning on talking over a club sandwich or not. It doesn't matter at this point.

I'm meeting him in an hour so we can fuck.

"You're drifting in daydream land, boss," my assistant, Gabriella, walks into my office. "I have to admit I'm right up there on cloud nine with you. Closing the Peterson file early calls for a drink. We should go out for lunch to celebrate."

Closing the Peterson file early was a relief for both Gabriella and me. I fought hard against the construction company that had unceremoniously fired Carl Peterson from a job that he held for more than thirty years. Their reasoning was thin and my case was strong.

I secured a substantial severance package for him that included the pension he'd been paying into for most of his adult life.

"I have lunch plans." I try to keep a straight face since Gabi and I are more friends than boss and employee.

She looks me over, her brown eyes pinned to my mouth. "You're holding back a grin. What are you doing for lunch? Is it business or pleasure?"

"You won't believe me if I tell you." I tip my chin up. She takes that as an invitation to sit in one of the chairs facing my desk.

She crosses her long legs. "You have to tell me now, Chloe. Where the hell are you going at noon?"

Visually, Gabi is the complete opposite of me. She's tall with dark hair and an olive complexion. She's also the ideal assistant since she has the ability to calm down every potential client who comes through the door.

Most people who seek out my services are trying to wage a battle against their current or former employer. They're typically angry and hell-bent on revenge. Gabi reassures them so that I can talk reason into them.

"I met a man at Leanna's wedding."

Her brow furrows. "Is he someone famous?"

I laugh as I skim through the inbox folder on the open laptop that's on my desk. "He's not famous although he's good-looking enough to be in the movies."

"So, he's not famous? Explain to me why I wouldn't believe that you met a hot guy at a wedding. Don't tell me it's someone I know. That's it, isn't it? You two started talking about your lives and put two-and-two together and he's one of my exes."

I take a second to absorb all of that. Gabi's personal life has put mine to shame the past two years. She's all about taking chances and if she feels there's no spark within the first hour of meeting a man, she'll let him know.

I admire that about her. She sees the value in every second that life gifts her with and she uses it to her full advantage.

How am I supposed to know if Evan is one of her exes? The chances may seem slim on the surface, but there's always a possibility. "Do you know anyone named Evan?"

"Evan?" she asks quietly. "The guy you met is named Evan?"

I trust that's his name although it could be anything. I'm still hiding behind a fake name. I have no idea if he's doing the same thing. "Yes. Evan. He looks like he's in his early thirties with brown hair and gorgeous blue eyes."

She runs the tip of her index finger over her bottom lip. "I've never met an Evan. He sounds hot. Are you two getting together for lunch?"

The details of my mid-day meeting with Evan aren't important. If I tell Gabi that I'm going to hook up with him before my two o'clock conference call, I'll spend the rest of the day evading a barrage of questions.

"We are," I answer truthfully before I try to deflect. "Can you have the Cooperman file on my desk when I get back? I want to go over it before my call at two."

She leans back in the chair, her gaze narrowing. "I'll handle it, but after that call is over, we're going to talk more about Evan and lunch."

We'll see about that.

Keeping details about Evan to a minimum means fewer complications and interference from my well-meaning friends and family.

It also means I can keep what's between us purely physical and after what I've been through the past few years, that's exactly what I need.

Chapter 11

Chloe

I step into the lobby of the Bishop Hotel at noon. It's busy. There's a line of people waiting to either check-in or out. I assume it's to check out since every hotel I've ever stayed in wants its guests to clear their rooms by twelve o'clock so they can ready them for the tourists who arrive later in the day.

I scan the faces of the people waiting to approach the reception desk. Evan isn't there. I glance over at a small seating area. There are two leather sofas and three chairs. Four people are gathered there, but they're all women.

As I turn in a circle to take in the entire lobby, I glance at every dark-haired man that I see. Not one of them is Evan. The excitement that has been buzzing inside of me since I saw him this morning starts to fade.

He might have stood me up.

The thought of Evan bailing on me after our conversation this morning stings.

I know that I wasn't imagining the way he was looking at me. There was hunger in his eyes when he saw me. He wanted me as much as I wanted him.

I start toward the lobby doors, intent on getting my ass back to my office where life is safe and predictable. I'm in control there. I know how to do my job and at the end of each day when I get home to my apartment, I'm content.

Maybe my life is as dull as watching paint dry. At least, I know what to expect almost every minute of every day.

"Jane?" A female voice calls from the left.

I ignore it because the only person who refers to me that way is Evan.

Just as I feel a light tap on the shoulder, the woman repeats the name. "Jane. You're Jane, aren't you?"

Before I can say another word, a bouquet of bright flowers is shoved into my hands.

"Evan told me to find the most beautiful blonde woman in the lobby, so you have to be her."

I take the flowers before I look at the woman next to me. She's a blonde too, the same height as me with blue eyes and a cheerful grin. She's dressed in a white wool coat, black pants and knee-high black boots.

"You're her, right?" She skims her fingers over her chin. "He didn't have a picture of you, but the description he gave me was spot-on."

I look around, not exactly sure what I'm searching for. "Where's Evan?"

"He's at the ..." she stops herself mid-sentence. "Evan was called into work. I'm Vanessa, a friend of his. He asked me to come by and give you these."

My gaze drops to the flowers in my hand and a white envelope that is tucked into the top of the bouquet. I tug it out from between the fragrant blossoms.

There's only one word written on it in blue ink.

"Jane."

"I need to get back to work." Vanessa slides on a pair of black leather gloves. "I'm glad I found you. Evan told me not to come back until the flowers and note were in your hands, so my work here is done."

***

I read the note Evan wrote me for a third time.

His handwriting is messy and uneven. The ink trails from one word to another but I can make out the message just fine.

"Jane,"

If I were an accountant or a lawyer who takes a normal lunch break, my cock would be in heaven right now.

Inside of you – heaven – that's how good it feels.

Look, my life is controlled by fate.

It calls. I run like the wind.

Fate called today.

I'm sorry that her timing is completely fucked up.

I'll be back at the Roasting Point Café the first chance I get.

Don't give up on me.

I like your beautiful face and the rest of you.

Evan (That is *my* real name, "Jane.")

P.S. I'm going to fuck *your* real name out of you the next time we're together.

"Chloe?" Rocco asks as he walks into my office. "Why is it that our father sees fit to send you flowers on a Thursday for no reason? Do you know how many flower arrangements the old man has sent me? Zero."

I laugh as I tuck the note back into the envelope and shove it into the pocket of my black dress. "He signed you up for that craft beer of the month thing for Christmas. I didn't get that. Do you hear me complaining?"

"Duly noted, counselor." He settles into one of my office chairs. "Gabi said you were free so I came right in. You're not busy, are you?"

I'm not. I stopped to pick up a turkey sandwich and a fruit salad on my way back to my office after I left the hotel. The flower bouquet I was carrying around the streets of Manhattan caught a few quizzical looks.

It's cold enough outside that I know the flowers will wither and die within a day, but for now, they're in a vase that Gabi found in her desk drawer. I put them on the windowsill next to my desk so they'll fall into my vision line every time I look out at the view of the building next door.

I can't afford an actual view, so I've grown accustomed to the red brick façade that greets me when I open the metal blinds each morning.

"I'm never too busy for you."

Rocco rolls his hand in the air. "For you, my favorite brother. You forgot to finish your sentence."

I don't have a favorite. Rocco is the one I feel most comfortable talking to about life stuff, but even that has a limit.

"I stopped by because I was in the neighborhood and Pop said some guy was giving you grief." He eyes the flowers. "Are those from him?"

I study his profile. I know he wasn't in the neighborhood. The words my father said to him are what brought him here. I barely even mentioned Evan to my dad the other night, but the Jones men are fiercely protective. This awkward conversation is proof of that.

"Your conference call is in five, Chloe." Gabi appears in the doorway. "I can entertain your brother while you take care of business."

Rocco turns back to look at her. "It's a tempting offer, Gabi, but I've got business of my own to handle. Maybe another time?"

There will never be a time when my assistant hooks up with my brother. She's always flirting with him and he tactfully shuts it down with a reasonable excuse and a killer smile.

"Everyone out." I motion to the doorway. "I'll talk to you later, Rocco, and tell dad I'm a big girl."

He stands and buttons his coat. "You're the baby of the family. You should be used to it by now. No man is going to hurt you again, Chloe. We won't let it happen."

I won't either. My heart is locked away and there isn't a bouquet of flowers or a handwritten note that will change that.

Chapter 12

Evan

You know what they say about best plans to get laid…or is it best laid plans?

If I wasn't the gentleman that I am, I'd say that Jane was the best lay I've ever had but I don't fuck and tell.

I missed my second chance today because of a complication with a patient who Jordan worked on last week.

Where was Jordan when the call for help came?

No one fucking knows so they called the only person they knew would hightail it across town and scrub in. Me.

I cursed as I left the Roasting Point Café and hopped on the subway.

It wasn't until I was at the hospital that the brilliant idea to send Vanessa on a mission to meet up with Jane hit me.

I took a chance when I asked Vanessa to handle picking up flowers for Jane. She agreed without question, so I wrote out a quick note, addressed it to Jane, and put some cash in my favorite nurse's palm.

"You're on fire today, Evan," Jordan, the bastard who turned his phone off earlier, walks into the staff locker room. "Two procedures in a row without missing a beat? Something tells me you're going to steal employee of the month from me."

I turn to look at him as I tug a T-shirt over my head. "Something tells me that you're an asshole. That something is reality. Where the fuck were you earlier?"

His gaze drops to the floor. "I took my mom to the airport. She hung around for a few extra days to make sure her baby boy is taking care of himself."

"You have a brother?" I deadpan. "Why didn't you answer your phone?"

He tugs his phone from his pants pocket. "The battery died. I didn't realize it was non-operational until an hour ago."

I'd call bullshit but I'm not wasting another minute in this place. I need sleep.

"You're covering my rounds in the morning." I pat him on the chest. "Don't bother trying to talk your way out of it. It's happening."

"I can handle that." He nods. "I'm in a particularly good mood since my date with Kylie is only days away."

Fuck, that's right. I forgot about my chaperoning gig in the cafeteria.

"You should get a trim before the big day." I jerk my chin up. "Kylie likes her men well groomed."

He rakes a hand through his bushy blond hair. "Good point. I'll take care of it. Mark my words, Evan, my date with Kylie is going to be the best thing that's ever happened to her."

Considering the fact that Kylie once graced the cover of three major fashion magazines in the space of year, I doubt that the upcoming mid-day rendezvous with Jordan and I will even rate in her *'worst hours of my life'* list. It'll be nothing but a distant memory to her before the clock strikes one.

"My rounds, Jordan." I remind him with an elbow to his side. "Handle it, or I'll tell Kylie your dick is a hairy beast."

"He is a beast." He grabs the front of his khaki-colored pants and squeezes whatever bulge is there. "And Kylie is the beauty."

"That's so fucked up," I mumble as I walk away.

I'd bail on that lunch but it was Jordan's generosity that gave me the chance to hook up with Jane. I owe him a lot more than he asked for, but he doesn't need to ever know that.

***

"Thank you for the flowers."

I stare at her mouth. Jane is wearing a very light pink tinged lip-gloss this morning. It makes her lips look plump and kissable and if we weren't standing in the middle of this crowded café, I'd be tempted to kiss her so I could get a taste of the gloss and her.

"You're welcome," I answer as I trail my gaze up to her eyes. They're outlined with less makeup tonight than the night we met. Her nose is red at the tip from the winter wind outside and the collar of her coat frames her delicate neck.

I've never noticed the small details about any woman before, but with Jane I soak it all up and store it in my memory.

"I'll get you a coffee. What name should they write on the cup?"

"Jane."

I arch a brow. "That's not your name."

"You don't know that." Her eyes drop to my chest and the open top button of my coat. "For all you know my name is Jane Smith."

As much as I like the game, I need to know her name. "Your voice changes every time you say it. You know that, right? It's higher. It's a sure sign that you're lying through your perfect teeth."

"Are you a policeman?" She tilts her head as she studies my face. "Is that why you had to take off yesterday? You had a big case to solve?"

"You're deflecting," I avoid her questions with ease. "Tell me your real name."

She scans the space near us before she leans in to whisper to me. "Your note distinctly said that you were going to…well you mentioned a particular method for getting my name out of me."

I almost meet her mouth with mine when I move forward. I resist the urge to kiss her and instead I rest my lips against her ear so I can speak in a hushed tone. "I'll clarify so there's no misunderstanding. In the letter I wrote that I'm going to fuck your real name from you. I'll hold you on the brink until you tell me and when you do, I'll make you scream my name again."

"That won't happen." She inches back so she can look me in the eye. "You may be great in bed, but it's just sex and I always keep my wits about me. I have more self-control than most people."

"Let's test that now, shall we?"

"Now?" Her gaze narrows. "I have a job to get to. I can't just go to a hotel with you right now."

"Live a little, *Jane*," I stress the last word. "Push back whatever the fuck you have planned this morning and prove me wrong. Show me that you can walk out of the hotel room without giving me your name."

"That sounds like a dare," she pauses. "Are you daring me to prove that I have self-control even during sex?"

"I am," I confirm with a nod of my chin. "Come with me now and when we fuck, we'll see if your self-control is as strong as you think it is."

"This is insane." She reaches into her briefcase and pulls out her phone. "I have to text my assistant to tell her I'll be an hour late."

I stall her hand when I reach for her wrist. "Two or three hours late, Jane. Your self-control has no chance against me."

She yanks her hand free and types out a message. "You're wrong, Evan. I'm stronger than you think."

Chapter 13

Chloe

"Chloe! Oh my, God. My name is, it's, please. It's Chloe."

Evan stops. He just stops mid-lick to look up at me. "Chloe? Did you say your name is Chloe?"

I nod while I try to focus on his face. He's been eating my pussy for the past thirty minutes.

My god, he's talented, or at least his mouth is.

"It suits you perfectly." His tongue swipes his bottom lip. "It's as beautiful as you are."

I appreciate the compliments almost as much as I appreciate the two orgasms I already had. I was tearing toward a third when he decided to ask me what my name was for the fifth time.

I gave in because I wanted to come again. Now, I'm aching for it and he's resting his lips against my thigh. His mouth is too far from where I really want it to be.

I wiggle my ass on the bed to try and draw his attention back to my core.

He moves, not toward it but he pulls back and kneels on the bed. He's shirtless, but still wearing the jeans he had on when we arrived at the hotel room.

I waited while he booked us a room. It's early, so the only people walking through the lobby were visiting business people with their eyes trained on their phones.

It's not as if I would have cared if anyone would have noticed me waiting for Evan. I'm single and if I want to start my day with a literal bang, I can.

I might have to do this more often.

This is the first time I've ever had morning sex and I don't intend on it being the last time.

"I brought some condoms." Evan makes that announcement as he slides to his feet. "I realize that you need to get to work before the day is over, so we'll use one today and save the rest for next time."

He strips his jeans and boxer briefs off quickly revealing his thick, hard cock. The man is rock solid in every way possible. His body is sculpted and strong.

The empty condom package hits the carpeted floor as he sheaths himself.

"How many times did it take, Chloe?" His voice is low and measured.

I close my eyes to try and hide the unrestrained need that I know he can see in them. "How many times did it take for what?"

I feel the bed shift under his weight. He crawls over my legs before he settles above me. "Open your eyes."

I peek out of the corner of my left eye. My God. The man is like a mythical beast whose purpose is only to draw pleasure from women.

His hair is a mess from where I tangled my fingers in it. His top lip is wet and I instantly wonder if it's from his own perspiration or from me. He didn't hold back when he licked and sucked me. He used his lips, his tongue, his teeth and three of his skilled fingers.

"Open your eyes," he repeats in a rough growl. "I want you to look at me when I fuck you."

Holy hell. This is so much better than gossiping with Gabi before my first appointment of the day.

"Maybe I like to do it with my eyes closed." I drape my hand over my eyes.

I feel his breath skirt over my cheek before he kisses me softly on the lips. "You don't. I caught you looking at me last time. Go ahead and pretend you're shy. We both know you like looking at me when my cock is deep inside you."

I almost moan aloud.

As he inches his cock closer to my core, I slowly open my eyes. He's staring at me.

My breath catches when he slides his cock inside. "You're so…"

"Deep inside of you," he interrupts with a low groan. "And it feels so fucking good."

He thrusts even deeper and I raise my hips from the bed to meet his every movement. It feels like perfection. It's as if we were meant for only each other.

"God, Chloe, your body…" His voice is a strangled sound as he slams into me, over and over, harder and harder until I arch my back because I feel it coming. I shiver with the electricity racing up my body, capturing me, taking me closer and closer to the edge.

"You're going to come," he whispers as he looks deep into my eyes. "Keep going. Just feel."

I do. I come hard and as when he hears me say his name, he loses all control and fucks me with long, solid strokes until he orgasms with a shudder and a grunt.

***

"Where do you work?" He adjusts the collar of my white blouse.

I stare into his face. He's dressed now, but his hair still has that '*I just fucked Chloe look*.' It suits him. "At a place."

"Has anyone ever told you that you're short on the details?" He brushes his soft lips over mine. "Lick your lips and you'll taste sweetness."

I smile. I like that he's so comfortable talking about sex. "Where do you work?"

He looks down his nose at me. "At a different place than you do."

"At a gym?" I pat his abs through his sweater. "You look like you could be a fitness model."

"Is that a thing? Do people earn money doing that?"

I shrug. "You would. You're in really good shape."

"I happen to like the shape of you more." His large hands slide down my sides before he moves them to cup my ass through my black skirt. "I need to bite this the next time I see you. You have a perfect peach of an ass."

"Are you an ass man?" I wiggle mine against his hands.

He moves to lower his mouth to mine again. "I'm a man who likes your ass and every other part of you."

We kiss. It's slow and sensual. His tongue inches my lips apart and I taste him, me and every chance I've never taken until now.

Maybe being spontaneous and adventurous isn't that bad after all. How can it be when a gorgeous man is kissing me like the world outside this room doesn't exist?

Chapter 14

Evan

"You have something on your face," Jack Pearce says as I lower myself into the chair across from him in the hospital cafeteria.

I scrub my hand over my chin. "I ate a bagel twenty minutes ago. You'd think my best friend wouldn't give two shits that I'm sporting a crumb or two. We can't all look like we stepped out of the pages of GQ magazine."

He squints at me. "I was talking about the fact that you're smiling. When's the last time you had a grin on your face in this place?"

It's not often.

My bedside manner is impeccable. I'm charming-as-fuck, and I try to keep things light between my patients and me, but I'm dealing with heavy shit on an hour-to-hour basis.

Being cheery isn't a job requirement when you work in Manhattan's busiest hospital.

"If I'm indeed smiling it has nothing to do with this place, and everything to do with Chloe."

He looks down at the paper cup in front of him that's half-filled with coffee. "Who is Chloe?"

"Chloe is Jane."

That draws his gaze up to my face. He's clean-shaven, black-haired and his eyes have been called everything from piercing to intense. I'd call them green, but the women who have hit us up when we're grabbing a beer often say they get lost in them. All I'm seeing in them right now is curiosity.

"You finally got her name out of her?"

I don't dive into the details of how I spend the early part of my day. I'm still riding the high of my rendezvous with Chloe.

I pushed her to give me her number once we were back in the hotel lobby, but she held firm. She's wounded. I see it when I look at her. Some idiot fucked her over and made her wary of every other human being with a dick.

After we'd played a back-and-forth game about whether she'd give me her number, I dropped it, kissed her and told her to keep getting her coffee at Roasting Point. My schedule is jam-packed for the next three mornings, but I'll get back there to see her as soon as I can.

"I got her first name," I confess. "It's a start."

"You like this woman, don't you?" He tips the coffee cup toward me before he takes a mouthful.

I shrug. "I do. I don't know what it is about her, but I like being around her."

"Have you two been hanging out? I didn't think your work would leave you time for a mistress."

That old fucked up joke about me being married to my work started the day I graduated from med school. When we met years before on a college campus, we hit it off even though I was knee deep in my studies and he was coasting through business school.

Now, he runs a boutique financial services company.

Jack keeps people's finances fit, and I keep their bodies healthy.

"I've seen her a couple of times now." I nod. "We both go to the same coffee shop."

He looks around the crowded hospital cafeteria. "I thought you got your coffee here. You seem fond of this particular blend of swamp water."

I laugh. "It's not that bad, Jack. I don't meet Chloe here. It's at a Roasting Point Café uptown."

"She has excellent taste." He pushes back from the table. "I came down here to see if you were still alive and kicking. You could answer your phone sometime."

I stand because I know he's got a meeting three blocks away in ten minutes. He told me as much when I finally answered his call an hour ago while I was between patients.

"We'll get together for a beer when I get a night off." I round the table to hug him. "You've fallen a notch or two on my priority list, Jack. Don't take offense, but you're not as pretty as Chloe."

He pats me on the back as we break the embrace. "I worry about you. I have to say I'm glad you finally have your eye on something other than your career. Maybe I can meet Chloe sometime?"

Considering the fact that I don't know her phone number, her surname or where she works, I doubt like hell I'll be setting up a meet-and-greet with her and my best friend anytime soon.

"I don't want to scare her away." I step back. "I'm letting Chloe set the pace on this, so I'll take it as slow as she needs me to."

"You're smarter than you look." Jack buttons his suit jacket.

"Fuck you too, Pearce. Fuck you too." I wave a hand as I walk away.

***

I step into my apartment after midnight. It's cold, so damn cold because I turned the heat down when I left this morning. I see no reason to pay to heat this space when I'm not in it.

I toss my coat on the back of my worn leather sofa and walk toward the radiator. I live in a pre-war building. In this city that can mean one of two things; the first is that you're paying too much rent on a space that someone has invested a lot of money in to fix up.

In my case, it means that a shitty landlord did bare minimum repairs before he rented the apartments out for a little less than premium.

The building is what it is. I knew that when I moved in. I'd rather sacrifice luxury for less debt and a savings account. I'm comfortable here. It provides me a place to come to where I can be at peace.

I need that. I especially needed it today after the afternoon I had.

Complications in surgery are never a good thing. I prefer the coast from incision to last suture, but today wasn't like that.

I spent three hours trying to save the leg of a woman with diabetes. I didn't win this one and fuck if that still doesn't piss me the hell off.

She'll learn to adapt and I'll come to accept that you can't always get what you want in life.

The patient knew the chances of success were slim but she trusted me to do my best. I did. Fuck, if it wasn't enough today.

I toss my phone on my bed before I strip out of my clothes so I can hit the shower. I wish I had Chloe's number. I want to call her even though she knows nothing about me other than how I fuck.

I scowl and curse under my breath as I walk out of my bedroom and leave behind the regret that I didn't push harder for her number.

Chapter 15

Chloe

I look at Gabi. She's dressed impeccably tonight. Once a month we go on a 'friend date.'

We always pull an idea out of a coffee cup that sits on Gabi's desk. It's filled with small pieces of paper that are labeled with different activities.

Two months ago we went bowling. Last month we saw a romantic comedy at the movies and tonight we're out for dinner.

It's Gabi's treat and judging by the prices on the menu; I'm paying my assistant a very generous salary.

"What do you want to drink, Chloe?" Gabi eyes me over the top of the menu. "I'm going full-on Cosmo tonight."

"I'm good with the water." I look up at the server standing next to the table. He's been back twice to get our drink order and each time Gabi has waved him away with a swat of her hand while she debated between a Cosmopolitan and a Martini.

"Water?" She rests the menu on the table. "I thought we'd share a toast. You have to get something stronger than water."

I shake my head. "I need to be in court first thing tomorrow morning. You know how I get when I drink. I'll feel groggy and I have to be on my A-game."

"That's a valid point." She tosses me a curt nod before she looks at the server. "One Cosmo for me and my friend will nurse that glass of water."

He smiles before he takes off toward the back of the restaurant.

"Did you get laid before work yesterday, Chloe?"

I drop the breadstick that I just picked up. Crumbs scatter all over the pristine white linen tablecloth and tumble onto the lap of my navy blue dress. "What? Why would you ask me that?"

"You were all…" Her voice trails as her hand waves in the air in front of me. "You were all flush and glowing when you got into the office and I didn't have a chance to ask you about it before you left for your meeting with that new client."

I tried to avoid eye contact with Gabi yesterday morning after I slept with Evan. She can read me like a book and the last thing I wanted was to waste the day away gossiping about my early morning rendezvous in a hotel room.

"I'm not dropping this." She eyes up her freshly manicured fingernails. "I want to know. Were you late yesterday because you were in bed with some guy or not?"

I'm saved briefly when the server arrives with her drink. She takes a tentative sip before she gifts him with a brilliant smile. "This is the best Cosmo I've ever had."

He winks as if he's responsible for it. He picked it up from the female bartender before heading over here. "Maybe when I get off work I can buy you another one?"

She pretends to mull it over with a deep sigh. "What time were you thinking, handsome?"

"Midnight," he answers quickly as he moves closer to her. "We can meet here, or I can grab your number and shoot you a text. Your choice."

Gabi has a plan of her own. It's a trick she taught me early in our friendship if I was semi-interested in a guy, but not entirely committed to going out with him. "Why don't you give me your number so I can send you a text later tonight?"

He's all over that idea. He starts calling out his digits before Gabi even has her phone in her hand. I watch in silence as she keys in the numbers before she looks up at him again. "I need your name."

"Trevor," he whispers under his breath. "What's your name?"

Her gaze drops back to her phone. "I'm Gabriella and that's Chloe."

Naturally, he doesn't look in my direction at all. I pick up the glass of water and take a drink while my stomach rumbles for more. I last ate hours ago and that was only an apple. I'm famished.

"It's a pleasure meeting you, Gabriella." His hand shoots out toward her. "I'm looking forward to seeing you later tonight."

"Can you give us a minute to decide on dinner?" She ignores his offered hand along with everything he just said. "Come back around in five and we'll be ready to order."

He jumps into action and moves toward another table where a couple has just been seated.

"Are you going to text him?"

She pushes her phone toward me and I read what's on the screen.

Trevor, the server: thin moustache.

"I thought you gave up taking notes on the men you meet?" I laugh as I hand her back her phone.

"I never know when I'll run into a man I've already met." She drops her phone in her bag. "Besides, I made him feel good and we'll get excellent service."

"He'll be waiting with baited breath at midnight to hear from you."

She enjoys a leisurely sip of her drink. "If I have enough of these, I might grab a disposable razor for that god-awful moustache and meet him after all."

I look over the menu. "I'm going to have a steak. That's okay, right?"

"I'm all for feeding the hungry." She looks to where Trevor is standing near the bar before her gaze shifts back to me. "I'll drop the subject of where you were yesterday morning if you tell me if it's the same guy who arranged for the flower delivery."

"It's him," I whisper under my breath. "That's the guy."

"I'm glad you met someone." She reaches across the table to cover my hand with hers. "It's good to see you having fun."

"It is fun." I pick up another breadstick and grasp it firmly in my palm. "It's harmless fun and right now, that's exactly what I need."

Chapter 16

Chloe

"Do you want to hit up a museum on Saturday?" Rocco asks before he picks up the tea I ordered. "There's a new installation at the Whitney that I'd like to check out."

Art isn't something that interests me. Rocco happens to love it and since he can't find anyone else who is willing to spend hours in a museum with him, I'm usually the one who tags along.

I'm tempted to say yes, but I have an important case heading to trial next month so every spare second I have is devoted to work. "I'm going to be in the office all weekend. You can drop by after the museum and fill me in."

"And bring one of these?" He hands me a tall paper cup of green tea. "Maybe a pizza too?"

"With extra cheese and pepperoni?" I take a small sip of the hot liquid.

He swallows a mouthful of the coffee he ordered for himself. "I know how you like your pizza."

"How does she like her pizza?"

Rocco and I both turn at the sound of a male voice. I recognize it immediately.

I haven't seen Evan in more than a week-and-a-half. I've been by the café most mornings, although I had to rush past it twice last week when I was running late for meetings. I did stop briefly to peer in through the window and didn't spot him.

I was disappointed but that was quickly replaced with acceptance. Evan and I aren't dating. We fuck. It's as casual as any relationship between two people can be.

Rocco looks to me for reassurance that I know Evan. I give him a quick nod.

"I'm Rocco Jones and you are?" Rocco offers his hand to Evan who takes it without hesitation.

He shakes it while he studies my face before he finally looks back at my brother. "Evan. I'm Evan. It's good to meet you."

"You two know each other?" Rocco takes a leisurely drink of his coffee.

"Not as well as you two know each other." Evan's gaze is back on me. "I had no idea that Chloe liked pepperoni pizza."

"With extra cheese," Rocco adds.

Evan's brows rise. "I didn't mean to interrupt. I just wanted to say hi to you, Chloe, since we haven't spoken in a few days."

Eleven days. It's been eleven days.

"You're not interrupting." Rocco pats Evan's shoulder. "My sister has to get to work and I need to head out."

"Your sister?" A wide smile covers Evan's mouth. "Chloe is your sister?"

Rocco grins. "The best sister a guy could ask for."

Evan's shoulders relax. He looks relieved and that makes me smile. "What else can you tell me about, Chloe?"

My brother looks at me before he turns back to Evan. "Chloe will fill you in on everything she thinks you need to know. I can tell you that her brothers protect her at all costs."

I had no idea when I got out of bed this morning that my brother would be threatening my fuck buddy before I got to work.

"Brothers?" Evan ignores the veiled threat to dig for more personal details about me. "How many Jones brothers are there?"

"Three," I blurt out because I want this conversation to be over. "I have three brothers."

"I have none," Evan admits. "Consider yourself lucky, Chloe."

I do.

"It was good to meet you, Evan. I'm going to run." Rocco leans down to kiss me softly on the forehead. "I'll stop by on Saturday, Chloe. Call me if you need anything before then."

I watch in silence as he walks away before I turn back to face Evan.

"Chloe Jones," he says slowly as he takes one step closer to me. "It suits you well."

I don't correct him. There's no need to. I'm working on changing my surname back to Jones since Newell is a name I've come to loathe. I want to leave it and the all the memories of it behind.

***

"I don't have time to go to a hotel with you today," I say when Evan motions toward the door of the café. "I have a lot going on at work."

His gaze travels over my face. "We don't have to go to a hotel. I came here to see you. That's all. If you can give me five minutes right now so I can stare at you, I'm good. "

I can't contain a smile. "You're very charming."

"You're mistaking honesty with charming." He kisses me lightly on the cheek. "I was hoping I'd see you today. I've been putting in long hours at work. I did stop by a couple of times last week, but you were nowhere to be found."

I raise my cup in the air. "Here's to long hours at work. I've been swamped."

He taps his cup to mine before he takes a drink. "I have tomorrow off."

It doesn't take a genius to read between the lines of that statement. He wants to hook-up. I could use the distraction and there's nothing like an orgasm to do just that. "Name the hotel and the time."

Something shifts in his expression. "We could do that, but I was thinking about dinner."

"Dinner?" I cast my gaze down before I look back at him.

He just invited me to dinner. I'd classify that as an actual date. A rush of heat overwhelms me and I know that my cheeks must be turning a soft shade of pink.

Dammit, Chloe. Get a grip. It's just a date.

"If you're not comfortable with that, say so." He taps the middle of his chest. "It may bruise my heart, but I'll get over it."

I press the toe of my boot against the corner of the barista counter. I should say no. Dinner can lead to more and I'm carrying so much baggage that he'd get lost under it.

"One meal, Chloe," he goes on. "I didn't ask you to marry me."

I laugh. "I know."

"If you feel like having dinner with me tomorrow, meet me at The Hot Oven Pizzeria on Broadway."

I nod.

"I'll be there at around six." He gives me a chaste kiss. "I hope to see you there, Chloe Jones."

I don't say anything in response because my heart won't let me. I have more than a day to think about it. I just hope that tomorrow at six, I make the right decision.

Chapter 17

Evan

I slide my phone back into the front pocket of my pants. Why the fuck is there no trace of the Chloe Jones I've been fucking? I searched for more than ten minutes and I came up with nothing.

There are a lot of women named Chloe Jones. A lot. When I narrowed my search to those who lived in New York State, I still couldn't find her.

Not one of the images online for women with that name matches the woman I met outside the hotel. She's an enigma.

Her brother popped up on dozens of sites. He's a retired professional poker player. Naturally, not one of the articles I read about him mentioned his family.

"What's with you?" Jordan rounds the corner and approaches me. "You look like you're ready to bite someone's head off."

I'm disappointed, not pissed.

"You look like you're waiting for a flood." I gesture toward his pants. "Have you grown an inch or two since you had those hemmed? Nice socks, by the way."

He looks down at where a good three inches of his pale pink socks are on display between his shoes and the bottom hem of his black pants.

"My tailor made a mistake." He tries to tug down on the fabric covering his thigh. "He gave me a good deal so I thought, what the hell, who will notice?"

I shake my head. "Did you pop in to see Mrs. Walton?"

"I did." He moves closer to me when an orderly passes us pushing an empty gurney. "I concur with your diagnosis."

I pat him on the shoulder. "That's all I need to hear. I'll stop in to her room to discuss treatment options."

I start to move past him but he stalls me with a hand to my forearm. "You didn't need to play third wheel at lunch the other day. Kylie and I would have been just fine on our own."

He would have been, Kylie not so much.

She was nice to him; nicer than I thought she'd be but she cut the lunch short when she got a text message.

It stung Jordan. I could see it in his face and when he asked her to dinner in front of me, I cringed.

She didn't decline or accept. Instead, she said she'd get back to him.

It was an act of kindness that has spiralled out of control.

Jordan keeps hitting me up to ask Kylie when she'll have an answer to his dinner invitation. I keep telling him to wait it out because patience is a virtue.

It's not. It's generally a waste of time.

"Has she said anything about me?" he asks expectantly. "I mean, it's been days, Evan. She must have said something by now."

"Ask her yourself." I gesture behind him. "Kylie's headed our way and this is your chance. Talk to her."

He spins around to look down the corridor. Kylie is strutting toward us like the former model she is. She tosses us both a wave and a smile.

"Kylie." Jordan approaches her with quick, uneven steps. "You look beautiful today."

"Jordan." She looks him over before she locks eyes with me. "Evan."

"I was wondering…" Jordan starts before he stops to pull in a deep breath. "I'm just wondering if you've given any thought to having dinner with me one night when we can both escape this place."

She lets out a little laugh as she pushes her long dark hair back over her shoulder. "Is this dinner with just you, Jordan, or both of you? Are we talking about a twosome or a threesome?"

I almost throw up in my mouth at the mental image of Jordan without clothes.

"Evan isn't part of this." Jordan squares his shoulders. "I'd like to take you to Nova for dinner one night. Just you and me."

I should step away before she crushes every one of his dreams under her red stiletto, but I don't. I'm all for watching the crash and burn. I take my thrills where I can get them.

"In that case, I'd love to have dinner with you, Jordan."

Well, fuck.

Miracles do happen every single day in this hospital.

***

When I asked the hostess to sit me at a corner table in The Hot Oven Pizzeria she gave me a wink. That might have had to do with the fact that I told her I was meeting a beautiful woman for a pepperoni pizza with extra cheese.

I hope to hell that Chloe doesn't make a liar.

My gaze falls to my phone. I got here early and that was on purpose. I had the day off but that didn't stop me from going to the hospital to do unofficial rounds. That resulted with a little one-on-one time with my boss.

He wanted to know why I'm not seeing more patients at our luxurious office uptown. I wanted to know why his wife always squeezes her tits whenever I make eye contact with her.

Obviously, I didn't ask my question because… rent, food, subway fare.

I'm doing fine with the set up I have going on at the hospital. I see patients in the office twice a month. The rest of the time, I'm where I need to be and that's a few steps away from an operating room.

I glance at the door again. It's five after six and Chloe isn't in sight.

I can wait it out. I have faith that she'll show because I see the way she looks at me.

She might not have admitted it yesterday, but she was happy to see me in that café. I was happy to see her too.

I look over at a table next to me. It's a couple, years younger than I am. They're obviously on a first or second date. Their movements are awkward and their loud conversation is stunted.

It's not a match made in heaven but most in this town aren't.

"Evan, I'm here. I came."

I look up and smile. Chloe's standing next to the table, dressed in jeans and an oversized red sweater. Her coat is draped over her arm. The wide smile on her face tells me she's glad to see me.

She has no idea how glad I am to see her.

Chapter 18

Chloe

He stands and pulls me into a warm embrace. He looks as handsome as ever. He's dressed just as casually as I am in jeans and a black sweater.

"Sit, Chloe." He pulls on the back of a wooden chair that's next to where he was seated.

As I sit, he takes my coat from my hands and drapes it over his on the back of a third chair.

"Did you have any trouble finding the place?"

I shake my head as I take in the space. It's not packed, but there are enough diners to keep the servers on the move. "It was easy to find. I've never been here before though."

He doesn't seem surprised by that. Pizza is plentiful in New York City. You can eat a different slice every day for a month and still have hundreds more places to try.

"It's one of my favorites." He pushes the large menu in front of him aside. "I've never had the pepperoni with extra cheese so I'm looking forward to that."

I like that he remembers what my brother said about my favorite pizza. It's not a big deal, but it speaks to his attention to detail. I value that in my life. I have to pay attention to every small detail at work, but I do the same in my personal life. Details can make all the difference.

"I like your brother," he goes on. "Are the other two like him?"

I sigh. I had a feeling that he'd bring up Rocco and I was hoping there would be a way to effortlessly change the subject. I don't see that out now, so I answer truthfully. "They're all very different."

"Are you the youngest?"

I nod. "I am."

"I have an older sister," he offers to my surprise. "That was it's own special hell when I was growing up."

I feel some of the tension in my shoulders release. "Did she bully you?"

"Babied me," he corrects me with a soft tap on the top of my hand. "Whenever I'd turn around she'd be right there. I love her, but when you're a twelve-year-old trying to be a bad ass, you don't want your older sister watching your every move."

"I know that feeling." I laugh. "My brothers are overly protective. They've always tried their best to shield me from everything."

"Is that why Rocco was giving me the once-over? He saw me as a threat?"

I shrug as I look down at the table. "He doesn't want me to get hurt. He has yet to realize that I'm a grown woman who can take care of herself."

He takes my hand in his and circles my palm with the pad of his thumb. "It's good to have someone looking out for you. We all need that."

We do.

I sit back in my chair. "Does your sister still look out for you?"

He releases my hand and drops his in his lap. "Not as much anymore. She's got her own stuff going on."

I don't press. How can I? I'm not willing to share my secrets with him so I can't expect him to share his with me.

***

"There are a million secrets lurking inside of you, aren't there?" Evan skims his lips over my neck. "Tell me one, Chloe. Just one."

I look over at him beneath hooded eyes. We're in a hotel. This one was next to the pizza place. That had me immediately wondering if he chose that particular restaurant for dinner so we could enjoy each other for dessert. "What makes you think I have secrets?"

He traces my erect nipple with the tip of his index finger. "All I know about you is that your name is Chloe Jones and you fucked every last ounce of energy out of my body just now."

I could say the same for him.

We didn't waste a second once he closed the hotel room door. We both stripped quickly. There wasn't any need for foreplay. He knew that I wanted his cock and he happily pulled me onto his lap and let me ride him until I came.

When he flipped me over onto all fours and took me from behind, I screamed into the sheets on the bed. I couldn't control it. He was so deep and every grunt only drove me closer to another intense release.

"This has to be fair." I watch as he licks my nipple with a long, gentle stroke. A shiver runs through me. "If I tell you something about me, I expect you to tell me something about you."

He doesn't look at my face as he answers. "I can do that."

I debate about what to confess. Most of my secrets are buried so deep that I'd have to wade through a river of tears and pain to pull them to the surface. I decide on something intimate, but not revealing.

"You were my first one-night stand."

"I know." His fingers skim over my stomach to the top of my mound. He drags them across the seam of my pussy in the most painfully slow way. My thighs clench as I feel desire pool in my core.

"How did you know?" I ask breathlessly as he circles my clit with the pad of his thumb.

He finally looks into my eyes. "You were nervous. You looked scared. I was tempted to tell you to take more time to think it over."

I inch my hips off the bed to create more friction with his touch. "I wasn't scared. I was unsure. Why didn't you tell me to take more time?"

He keeps his gaze locked to mine as he increases the pace of his thumb. "I wanted you too much. I had to have you."

I close my eyes. It's all too intense. His words, his touch and the feelings that are crowding my common sense and urging me to let go.

Chapter 19

Evan

I've never seen a more beautiful sight in my life than Chloe letting go. Every time she's climaxed, I've watched her intently. This last time, I was in awe.

I was fingering her while she confessed that I was her first one-night stand.

It made me want to tell her everything. All of my past mistakes, my regrets, and every way I've allowed myself to be as vulnerable as she was being in that moment.

She didn't have to tell me that, but she chose to.

"You're not getting off that easy, Evan." She rolls on her side to face me. "You promised that you'd tell me something too."

I take in every curve of her body. I'm grateful as fuck that she didn't pull the sheet up to cover herself.

She lets out a sigh. "When you look at me that way, it makes me think you're going to fuck me again to avoid confessing a secret."

I palm my semi-erect dick. "Is that an invitation because I can go again?"

She swats her hand on my bare shoulder. "If your confession is a good one, a blow job might be in order."

My cock swells instantly and I give it a leisurely stroke. "I'm thirty-four."

Her tongue slicks her bottom lip. "I need more."

"I work in medicine." I swallow with that one because I learned early on that when a woman meets a cock she likes, she'd go to great lengths to track it down.

That unwelcome awakening came one night when I was paged to emergency because a woman I'd fucked a week before had come in with a pain in her pussy that only '*Evan with the blue eyes*' could treat.

I have yet to live that down.

Chloe slides her hand along my thigh until she's inching my fingers out of the way to grab my dick. "You have one hell of a bedside manner."

I groan when she slides her palm up and down in steady, even strokes. "I could say the same for you."

"Are you a doctor?" She follows that question up with a dip of her head and a soft lick to the tip of my cock. "What's your last name, Evan?"

I part my lips to confess that it's Scott. I don't give two fucks if she knows my name, my address and my social security number.

I'd give her anything for the chance to shoot my load down her throat.

All I can manage is a guttural growl when she takes me in her mouth and moans around my dick.

***

"Evan, we need to talk." Jordan steps in front of me just as I'm about to slip out of the locker room after a twelve-hour shift.

I've been pulling long days since I saw Chloe a week ago. As much as I want to exchange numbers with her, I didn't ask.

I'm not one for analyzing myself but I hate the bitter sting of rejection and after the mind-blowing sex we had, I'd be bruised if she would have shut me down by not giving me her number.

I let her walk out of that hotel room with a kiss and nothing more. I haven't been back to the Roasting Point Café since that night. Since she hasn't shown up here at the hospital, I take that to mean that she didn't bother to drop by the hospital reception desk looking for a tall, dark and handsome doctor named Evan.

She might have done an online search but that would have netted nothing. I don't do social media and I'm not listed in the online directory at the private practice I work at because my boss sees me as a rank amateur even though I have more skill than he'll ever possess.

"What do you want, Jordan?" I glance down at his canary yellow socks. "I see that your tailor is still up to his old tricks."

"These are the same pants I was wearing last week." He shakes a leg. "I can give you his number. I'll have you know that I scored wearing this very outfit."

"Scored what?" I roll my hand in the air with impatience. "What exactly did you score other than a draft up your pant leg?"

"Kylie and I did it."

The concept is so foreign that I push aside the suggestion that he had sex with Dr. Newman. "You did what with Kylie?"

He cocks a brow and winks at me.

I scowl because that's about as fucked up as life can get. "You slept with Kylie?"

"Neither of us slept if you know what I mean." He elbows me in the side. "I need to tell you what happened while that was going on."

I tug a gray hoodie on as I shake my head. "You need to shut the hell up. I don't want to hear it, Jordan. Have a little respect for Kylie."

He laughs. "I'm not going to tell you how good it was, Evan, and it was good."

"You just did you bastard." I push past him. "I have to face Kylie on a daily basis. I don't think she'd appreciate the fact that I know about her sex life. She's like a sister to me, Jordan."

He grabs my shoulder just as I'm about to take another step. "The condom broke."

I look back at his face. "It happens. Kylie seems like the type to use backup protection."

He doesn't respond right away. Instead, he studies my face. "You don't get it. The condom broke because it was old, Evan. It expired three years ago."

I break out into a low chuckle. "You could have picked up a fresh package on your way to dinner, man. Why in the hell would you use a rubber that old?"

He inches his face closer to mine. "I haven't bought a package in years. I always carry one in my wallet. The one I was using with Kylie was the second in the pack."

I scan his face slowly putting two-and-two together.

Fuck.

"You had the first one, Evan." He points out the obvious. "I'm sure it's fine and all, but I wanted to give you a heads-up."

I scrub my hand over the back of my neck doing the mental math on when I first fucked Chloe. I have no clue what her cycle is and whether she's missed a period or not.

"I need to go." I stalk toward the exit of the locker room hoping like hell that the condom I used with her held strong and that she's taken care of birth control on her end.

Chapter 20

Chloe

I sit at my desk and stare out the window at the building next door. I could draw the pattern of bricks in my sleep. There's nothing unusual about it, but it's familiar and that's something that I've always needed in my life.

"You're daydreaming again?" Gabi steps into my office. "This Evan guy must be something else."

He is.

I haven't seen him in days but that hasn't stopped me from thinking about him on an hourly basis.

I used the sparse details I know about him to try and locate him online. I came up empty handed. After I searched for doctors named Evan, I broadened the scope of my mission to uncover his identity.

Combing through the staff directories at a few of the hospitals in the city was futile. It didn't take me long to realize that I have no idea whether he's a doctor or not. For all I know he's an x-ray technician or an orderly.

I don't care what he does for a living. I doubt that he cares what I do.

"I like him," I admit when she takes a seat in front of my desk. "We have a lot of fun together."

She tugs at the bottom of her hair. "Are you dating him or is it more of a casual thing?"

"Is that a diplomatic way of asking if we're sleeping together?"

She sits up in the chair, crossing her legs at the knee. "You haven't talked about him a lot and I know from the security guard in the lobby that you're here past ten on most nights, so I'm assuming that your time with him is limited to time spent in bed."

"You'd make a great detective." I laugh as I lean back. "That's exactly what it is. We meet to hook-up."

"And you're fine with that?" Curiosity laces her words.

"That surprises you?" I volley back. "Why does it surprise you?"

She heaves a sigh. "Your track record."

Those words should sting but they don't. She doesn't mean it as an insult. She's stating the truth. "Sometimes a person needs to try out a new track. I'm doing that with Evan."

The corners of her mouth rise. "A new track is exciting but sometimes it comes with twists and turns we can't predict."

"Isn't that part of the adventure? You see where it takes you and you can take one of those turns if you want to get off that track and onto a new one."

"You've never had a fuck buddy, Chloe." She grips the arm of the chair in her hand. "The number one rule is not to invest your heart in that person."

I scoff at the idea that I'm doing that. "I'm keeping my heart locked up tight. This is fun and that's all it is."

She pushes to stand. "Feelings have a way of showing up when you least expect them to. Don't lose sight of that. The last thing you need is to be hurt again."

"You know that I love that you look out for me but I'm a big girl and I'm going to enjoy the fun of this while it lasts."

"I'm always here if you need me. Just remember, that life is unpredictable even if you think you're on the right track."

***

I smile when I see Evan approach me in the café.

After my discussion with Gabi yesterday, I saw Rocco for dinner. I'd bailed on our pizza date so I thought I'd invite him out for a burger to catch up.

I needed the sibling bonding time and when he asked about Evan, I reiterated what I told Gabi but with much less graphic detail.

Rocco understood that it's casual and he encouraged me to keep doing whatever felt right for me.

Since I value his opinion more than anyone else's, I went to sleep last night feeling at peace with where my life is headed, both professionally and now, personally.

"Chloe, we need to talk." Evan stops short of where I'm standing.

I look him over. He's dressed differently today. He's wearing dark slacks and a white button down shirt under a dark blue blazer.

It's still cold outside so I'm surprised that he isn't wearing his wool coat.

I doubt that he's here to break up with me since we're not officially anything but people who meet for a good time.

"What do you want to talk about?" I take a small sip of my tea. "Do you want to grab a coffee first? The line is short right now."

He looks toward the counter where two baristas are busy stacking cups. "No. I'm not having a coffee."

The nervous energy that is bouncing off of him is palpable. I feel my stomach flip-flop. "What is it?"

He grabs me by the elbow to lead me over to a vacant table near the door. I don't have time to sit, but I do because it's obvious that this discussion isn't going to be short and sweet.

"I need to ask you something personal." He rubs his temples with his fingers. "I'm sorry I have to do this, but I haven't slept all night and I'm not the kind of guy who sees value in beating around the bush."

I rest my tea on the table when I realize that I'm shaking. "All right. I'll try and answer."

He closes his eyes before they pop open and lock with mine. "Are you late?"

I breathe a sigh of relief. "I have another five minutes before I need…"

"No," he blurts out. "I don't mean today. Are you late?"

I suck in a deep breath. "Am I late?"

He rests both hands together in the middle of the table. "Chloe, I am asking if you've missed your period."

I hang my head. Why the hell would he ask me that? Why?

"Chloe, I need to know. The condom might have broken that first night. I found out yesterday from the guy I got it from that the package was years old. It might have failed and if you're late we need to talk about options."

Options? I wish I had *options*. I've longed for *options* for years but some of us don't have the luxury of *options*.

"I know you must be in shock," he goes on. "If we have to deal with a pregnancy, I'll help. I'll be there to discuss what is best for us both."

Tears sting the corner of my eyes. I shake my head from side-to-side wishing he would shut up.

"Say something," he pleads. "You can scream at me all you want but say something. Are you on the pill? Is your period late? Is there any chance that I knocked you up?"

I finally look up and into his face. I see nothing but panic and fear.

"There's no chance," I answer softly. "You didn't knock me up."

He bends his neck back and audibly sighs. "Thank, Christ. So you've had your period since that night?"

I'm not going to lie to him. He didn't have to tell me that the condom might have broke, yet he did. He deserves the truth from me too. "I haven't had a period since then."

He looks right at me. "That was weeks ago. You should have had your period unless you use something other than the pill for birth control."

"I don't use birth control."

His eyes widen. "We need to go get a test done. If you come with me I can have someone draw your blood and we'll have the results within the hour."

He's on his feet before the words leave my mouth. "No one needs to draw blood. I'm not pregnant, Evan."

"You don't know that." He holds out his hand to me. "I know you're scared but once we have the test results we'll know whether this is an issue or not."

"It's not an issue." I don't touch his hand. "Trust me when I say that there is no chance that I'm pregnant."

"How can you know for sure?"

"I'm infertile," I say under my breath so the entire café doesn't know my secret. "You have as much chance of getting pregnant as I do."

Chapter 21

Evan

"Are you sure?"

The look on her face tells me that it was a fucked up question. She doesn't answer immediately because why the hell would she.

She looks like I took her heart and ran over it with a bus. Why the hell didn't I approach this conversation with the same tact I use when talking to my patients?

"My ex-husband and I tried to have a baby for years." She takes a deep breath. "We tried everything and the doctors finally got us both to accept that I'll never conceive."

It's not my area of expertise but I know that some of the best fertility specialists in the country call Manhattan home. I'm tempted to ask for the name of her physician, but it would do me little good.

I'm a fucking doctor who is well aware of the ethics of patient confidentiality.

The fact that she was married catches me by surprise. She has to be a few years younger than me and marriage isn't even a mirage in my distant future yet.

"You have nothing to worry about." She pushes back from the table and stands. I see the unease in her hands when she reaches to pick up the cup of tea. "I'm not pregnant."

I'm relieved. I'd be lying if I said I wasn't, but I'm also curious about her history.

I walked into this café worried shitless that I was about to become a dad. Now, I want to know why she was so desperate to become a mom and who the fool was that let her slip away.

"I need to get to work now." She puts the tea back down. "I'm not thirsty anymore."

"Chloe," I say her name before I realize I don't know how to handle what just happened between us.

"I can't be late." She turns to her side. "Thank you for being honest about the condom. I'm sure there are a lot of guys who would have just disappeared."

Maybe. If there are men like that, they deserve a punch in the groin.

"You had a right to know. " I stand too, unsure if my legs are going to hold my weight. I feel anxious and confused. I don't know why I want to hold her, but my hands are aching to reach for her to pull her close.

She nods. "I'll see you around."

I don't respond. She's damn right that she'll see me around. I want to erase all the pain I see in her eyes. Something tells me that there are more secrets buried below the surface that she's aching to share.

***

"I thought you were on top of your game, Evan." Jack leans back on my sofa so he can rest his feet on my coffee table. "You didn't have a condom so you borrowed one from a guy who never gets laid?"

I laugh aloud. "He's gotten laid at least twice that I know of, but I assure you I'm not counting. He had a condom in his hand when I was desperate for one. You would have taken it too."

"Probably." He shrugs as he draws a pull from a bottle of beer. "Remind me again why we aren't at the hockey game?"

"You gave your tickets to me and I gifted them to the couple who live down the hall from me. "

"Christ, I'm a nice guy." He chuckles. "Why did you feel the need to give away more tickets that I've paid good money for?"

"The two guys who live down the hall got married over Christmas. They're working their asses off to get through med school. I know that drill so I gave them the tickets so they could at least have one night of fun."

"I'm not going to say you're wrong for doing a good deed, but I'd like to sit my ass in one of those seats at some point this season."

I turn on the television and flip through the channels until I land on the game. "Besides, we can watch from the comfort of my home. What's better than that?"

"A toast to the fact that you're still kid free." He holds up his bottle in the air. "Here's to dodging bullets."

I raise my bottle too. Jack doesn't need to know that Chloe can't conceive. I left that detail out when I told him that she's not pregnant. I wouldn't have mentioned it at all, but I made a frantic call to him last night after Jordan filled me in on his broken condom.

"Let's hope we avoid the parent trap for years." Jack tosses me a smile. "I know I'm not ready and there's no way in hell you should be parenting a kid."

I don't argue that point. I barely have my own life in order. A baby is the last thing I need.

Chapter 22

Chloe

Gabi follows me into my office. "Do you want to talk about anything? You know I can clock out for a few minutes and put on my best friend hat if you need me to."

"Your best friend hat?" I smile. "Is that different from your assistant hat because I was under the assumption that they were one in the same."

She twists her mouth into an over exaggerated frown. "You know what I mean. We can push aside all the work we need to go over and talk about what happened before you got to work yesterday."

"Nothing happened," I lie.

I didn't say a word to Gabi yesterday about my awkward conversation with Evan. I raced to my office after I left the café, trying to regain some of the composure I'd left behind.

I wasn't successful.

I breezed past Gabi's desk and slammed my own office door behind me.

She was on my heel and as quickly as I closed the door, she opened it back up with a demand that I tell her what was going on.

I couldn't. The words wouldn't form on my tongue so I waved her away with an excuse about a work problem.

She didn't buy it since she's the one I'm always confiding in when something goes wrong in the office.

"Gabi." I take a step toward her so I can hold her hands in mine. "I love that you're concerned about me but you don't need to be. I'm fine. It's nothing."

"If it was nothing you wouldn't have looked the way you did." She tilts her head so she can look me directly in the eyes. "I know you. Something happened that knocked your world off its axis. You know you can tell me anything."

I do know that. Gabi is one of the few people in my life I can say anything to and I know that she'll never repeat it.

The professional part of that is related to the non-disclosure agreement she signed when she started working for me. The personal side of that is based on the strength of our friendship.

I give in because I can tell by the look on her face that she's not going to let this go. "I saw Evan yesterday morning and we talked about some stuff."

"Evan and stuff, " she repeats back. "You need to give me more than that."

I smile. "It was really personal. He asked me intimate questions. We've done intimate things so why did it freak me out when he asked me intimate questions?"

"What questions?" The level of concern in her tone rises. "Does he want to try some kinky stuff that you're not sure of? I've done most everything so ask away if you need more info on any of that."

I cringe inwardly. "No, it's nothing like that."

"I'm not following, Chloe. You can just tell me what the questions were. I promise you're not going to shock me."

I know I won't. I doubt anything would shock her after the confession she just made.

I wait for a beat before I respond. "He was worried that the condom had broken on that first night we spent together."

"Did it?"

I shrug. "I didn't notice if it did. I showered when I got home and I...I just don't know."

"Has he been tested recently?" She moves closer. "We can go to my doctor right now for the tests. She'll fit you in."

"He was more worried about the possibility that I might be pregnant."

Realization washes over her expression. Gabi knows. She was one of the people who talked me through those years and helped me see the light at the end of the tunnel. "I'm sorry, Chloe. That had to have been rough for you."

"I told him," I admit. "I just came right out and told him why he didn't need to worry about me getting pregnant."

"You told him?"

I nod. "He was scared. I wanted to reassure him so I told him that I'm infertile."

"Did you tell him everything?" She scans my face. "Does he know what caused it?"

I shake my head briskly. "That's inconsequential. It doesn't matter why I can't have children. All that matters is that it's not possible."

"You're right," she says assuredly. "That's not any of his business."

It's not. I've been trying to convince myself of that fact since I walked out of the café.

Evan and I are casual lovers who had a short-lived scare. It doesn't change the fact that our relationship doesn't involve long conversations about the past.

He doesn't need to know the brutal details of what happened to me before we met. That's my past and it belongs to me. I have every intention of keeping it that way.

Chapter 23

Evan

I fucked up. I know it. I've juggled my schedule like a master the past three mornings just so I could get to the Roasting Point Café by eight sharp. I waited every one of those days for Chloe but she didn't show.

How the hell can I blame her for that? She's probably still in recovery mode after that conversation we had earlier in the week.

I dug up some seriously painful shit from her past all because I was desperate for the reassurance that I wasn't going to be on the hook for child support for the next eighteen years.

I could have been more sensitive, but I wasn't and since I can't hop in a time machine and make me way back to that morning, I did the next best thing. I tracked down her brother.

"Rocco." I offer my hand when he approaches. "It's good to see you."

He's surprised. I can't tell if it's because he recognizes me or not. He wasn't expecting me. Who expects to be approached by a virtual stranger mid-workout?

I wouldn't have known he'd be here except for the recent post he made on one of his social media accounts. It was exactly thirty-two minutes ago and since I had a break between a consult and surgery, I hopped on the subway and headed here.

"Evan, right?" He shakes my hand briskly. "Your choice of work-out attire is interesting."

I laugh that off since I'm dressed in scrubs and a black sweater. "I didn't know you were a member here too."

I know I'm stretching the truth. I did know he was a member. I happen to be one although the last time I stepped foot in this place was months ago.

I make a mental note to cancel my membership on my way out.

"Trying to keep the heart healthy." He rakes a hand through his hair. "Heart disease runs in the family so I'm taking a proactive approach."

He's a smart man.

"Hey, now that I ran into you, I have a question." My intention is to sound nonchalant. I can't tell whether that's working for me or not.

"What's that?" he asks before he takes a mouthful of water from a bottle in his hand.

I swallow, realizing that this is treading on dangerous ground. "I want to surprise Chloe with some flowers. I could use some insight into her favorite."

He smiles. "Pink roses. She loves them."

I like knowing that. I want to dig deeper but that will raise alarm bells. If he knew what happened between Chloe and me the last time we talked, I doubt he'd be giving me the time of day. "That's good to know. I'll pick up a bouquet for her today."

"Today?" He furrows his brow. "You don't think they'll be dead before you get a chance to give them to her?"

I try to act like I know what the fuck he's talking about. "Good point."

"Unless you're planning on sending them to her hotel in Boston. That's a surprise she'll appreciate."

With that he steps back onto a treadmill and starts a slow jog.

I walk away wondering why the hell she's in another city and whether she's thinking about me as much as I'm thinking about her.

***

"What's her name?"

I turn to look at the patient I'm having a consultation with. Physically there's absolutely nothing wrong with her. Emotionally, she's suffering from a broken heart.

Her symptoms began the day her husband died.

"Who?"

"The girl that you wish you could be talking to right now." Judith Lancaster points at my cell phone. "You've stolen a peek at that twice since you walked into this exam room. Might I suggest you take the bull by the horns and call her yourself?"

I take a seat on a stool that is facing the exam table. "I was checking the time. I'm not waiting for anyone to call me."

I'm not. I wish to fuck I was. Maybe if I had pushed Chloe for her number, I would know whether she's even back in Manhattan yet.

It's been days since I tracked her brother down at the gym. I sent Vanessa to the Roasting Point Café this morning with a bouquet of pink roses in her hand. Chloe didn't show and now those roses are sitting on the desk at the nurses' station reminding me that I know virtually nothing about a woman I think I'm falling for.

"My husband used to tell me that love begins in here." She taps her forehead before she lowers both hands to her chest. "And it lives in here."

I listen because I sense there's more to tell.

"You can't stop thinking about her." She leans forward to rest her forearms on her knees. "That means that it's still young."

"It's not like that." I stand and pick up my tablet to make note of our uneventful appointment. "You're fine, Judith. You can get back to your everyday activities."

She carefully steps down from the table, adjusting her pant legs in the process. "I may be fine to you, but my heart says something different."

"Grief can disguise itself in many forms." I snap the cover of the tablet shut. "Give it time. Only you can set the pace that works for you."

"The same advice applies to love." She smiles as she reaches past me to grab her purse. "You need to give it time. Only you can set the pace that works for you, but remember that no one lives forever."

I know that all too well. Grief is a larger part of my life than love has ever been. It may be time to change that.

Chapter 24

Chloe

"I can move all your appointments today," Gabi rests her palm against my forehead. "You don't feel warm. Maybe it's not the flu."

I shrug as I pull away from her. "My dad and I had seafood in Boston two days ago. His stomach has been uneasy too. Maybe that's all it is."

"That might be it." She starts toward my office door. "I'll go get you a warm ginger tea. That always helps when my stomach is acting up."

I nod as I watch her leave before I turn my attention to my laptop and the calendar app that lists my schedule for today.

It's lighter than I thought it would be. That's because a client who was set to launch a lawsuit against their former employer dropped it when they were hired back on.

That's not uncommon in my line of work and since I ask for an upfront retainer, I'm never working pro bono. I wish I could at times, but I have to live.

"Chloe?"

My head pops up when I hear Rocco's voice at my office door. I greet him immediately. "Hey, you. I haven't see you in at least a couple of weeks."

He steps in and takes off his scarf before slipping out of his wool coat. "How was the trip with dad? That was a last minute thing, no?"

It was. I needed some space after the conversation I had with Evan about the pregnancy scare. Since I had planned on heading to Boston early next month to interview a potential client who had recently relocated there from New York, I decided to ask my dad to tag along.

He was all over the idea and planned our entire schedule including fitting in my work commitments.

We both needed it and I came back to Manhattan feeling refreshed and recharged until I woke up this morning with an upset stomach.

"We had a blast." I smile. "You know how much fun it is to travel with him."

"I do." He nods as he takes a seat across from my desk. "Do you remember when I used to take him to Vegas with me when I was playing poker? I swear the man had more fun than I did."

I like hearing that. Our father is still grieving my mom's death. It was the second loss he suffered. His first wife died of cancer before Rocco's seventh birthday leaving my dad with three small boys to raise on his own.

"What brings you to my office?" I close the lid of my laptop. I need to be at the courthouse in thirty minutes so I'll have to cut my conversation with him short.

"Evan."

My brows pop up in surprise. "Evan?"

He nods briskly. "We ran into each other at the gym two days ago."

I bite the corner of my lip wanting to demand that he tell me about what they talked about, but knowing full well that it involves me.

Evan doesn't seem like the type of guy who would share personal details about our conversation with another person, especially my older brother. "I haven't seen him in awhile. How is he?"

"Fine." His voice lowers. "He wanted to know what you favorite flowers are. He didn't send a bouquet of pink roses to your hotel room in Boston?"

My heart thumps inside my chest. Rocco knew what hotel my dad and I were staying in because he was the one who suggested it since it was on the waterfront. Evan didn't send any flowers though, so my brother must have kept that information to himself.

"Some men prefer to hand deliver flowers," I offer even though the only flowers I've ever received from Evan were delivered by his friend, Vanessa.

"Either way, I see some pink roses in your not-too-distant future."

I tap the face of the watch on my wrist. "I see a court date in my very near future so I need to take off. You're welcome to stay and visit with Gabi."

He chuckles. "That one would eat me alive. I'll pass."

I laugh as I push myself to my feet. "Are you headed in the same direction as me? We can share a cab?"

"That's a plan I'm on board for. I'll take every minute I can get with my sister."

***

I tap my toe, wishing that the barista would fill the cup with hot water and hand the ginger tea I ordered to me. It's my third cup today. After Gabi shoved the cup into my hand as I was exiting the building with Rocco, I sipped it on my way to the courthouse. It helped almost instantly.

I picked up another on my way back to my office and I'm about to take yet another home with me. I make a mental note to stop at the deli by my apartment to see if they have a box of ginger tea bags. It would save me a fortune.

"Chloe." I feel a hand on my shoulder. "I have no idea you stopped in here at the end of the day."

I recognize Evan's voice instantly. I've missed it even if I didn't want to admit that to myself.

I turn to look at him. He has a light growth of beard covering his jaw but other than that, he looks exactly as he did the last time I saw him here.

"I had a break at work and thought that I'd come down here on the off chance, you'd walk past." He gestures toward the sidewalk outside the café. "When I looked in the window, I couldn't believe it was you."

I skim my hand over my hair. I didn't put a lot of effort into my appearance this morning because I was feeling under the weather. I showered quickly, pinned my hair up into a messy bun and chose a pair of black pants with a black blouse.

"How have you been?" I ask because I don't know what else to say.

He takes a measured step closer. "Worried about you. I didn't handle our conversation well. I should have been more sensitive. I'm sorry, Chloe."

Chapter 25

Evan

Her bottom lip quivers when I offer her my apology. She looks pale and tired. I won't tell her that because I've known enough women in my lifetime to know that some take offense when offered an unwanted opinion.

"You were scared." She looks into my eyes. "You did nothing wrong. Whatever I felt was because of stuff from my past. That's not on you."

She's kind. I pushed her to reveal details about herself that were incredibly personal. The woman doesn't know my last name or where I work yet I know that she's suffered through a painful experience in her pursuit to have a child.

"Let me make it up to you." I look over at the large paper cup that the barista is pushing toward her. "I can take you for something to eat."

Her hand falls to the front of her coat over her stomach. "My dad and I must have eaten some bad fish. We both picked up a trace of food poisoning. I'm sticking to tea for today."

I pick up the cup and put it in her hands. "Do you want to talk? I have a couple of hours before I need to be back at work."

She looks up at the circular clock that's hanging on the wall. "You have to go back to work at eight? You are a doctor, aren't you?"

I see no reason to hide behind a veil of mystery anymore. The scale of information between us is unbalanced. I need to right that. "I'm a surgeon."

Her gaze falls to my hands. "That's why you're so good with your hands."

I welcome the playfulness more than she could ever know. "They're gifted."

"I'd agree with that." She sips the tea. "This is hot. We can sit while it cools and then I'll head home."

I'll take it. The lead weight in my gut is finally disappearing. I know she's okay and willing to talk to me again. Suddenly, everything feels right in my world again.

***

"So you're a hockey fan?" I arch a brow. "Why does that surprise me?"

She exhales audibly. "I grew up in a home with three brothers and a dad who loves sports. I had no choice but to get invested in it."

I laugh. "When you put it like that, you probably know more about the sport than I do."

She circles her palm around the bottom of the cup in front of her. "I haven't followed it as closely as I used to. Work keeps me crazy busy."

It's an opportunity for me to ask the question I've been dying to. I have her pegged as an accountant or executive. She's always sharply dressed and I've never seen her in this café without her leather briefcase in her hand.

"What do you do for work, Chloe?"

Her eyes widen as she picks up the cup and takes a drink. She holds it next to her lips a moment too long. I know she's contemplating whether she should answer the question or not.

I rescue her because I don't want a repeat of our last conversation when I pushed for more than I should have. "If you're not comfortable telling me, it's not a big deal. I just keep imagining you as an accountant."

"An accountant?" She laughs through the question. "I'm not an accountant. I'm a lawyer."

A lawyer. It's impressive.

"You look surprised," she goes on. "I'm sorry that I had to destroy all those accountant fantasies you've been having."

It's my turn to chuckle. "Not a problem. I'll jerk off to images of you in a courtroom now with fuck me heels on and an attitude."

"Fuck me heels?"

I tilt my chin down. "You're wearing a pair today."

She is. They're red and high. Her shoes are the perfect accent to her black blouse and pants.

"I didn't realize they were called that." She leans back to cross her legs. "I'll be thinking about that the next time I wear them to court."

"What type of law do you practice?" I push for more because I crave details about her.

"It's my turn to ask a question."

I'm mildly disappointed that I didn't get more out of her, but I'm content. "Ask away."

She considers what she's going to say before she finally opens her mouth to speak. "Rangers or Islanders?"

I wasn't expecting that. I was prepared to tell her my last name when asked, but if she's more interested in which New York-based hockey team I cheer for, I'll tell her. "Islanders."

"Me too." Her mouth breaks into a wide grin.

I take a leap with my next question. "Do you want to go to a game with me sometime?"

"You're serious?" She props her elbows on the table. "I haven't been to a game in years."

"I'll make it happen."

I will. I'll grab a pair of tickets from Jack and convince Jordan to cover for me at work. I had no idea when I got to this café today that I'd be leaving with the promise of a second date with Chloe. Things are definitely looking up.

Chapter 26

Chloe

"Why haven't you asked him for his number?" Gabi bites into an apple. "I don't get it. You two are practically dating, Chloe. It's time for him to step up to the plate and hand over his number."

It doesn't bother me that I don't have Evan's number. I ran another search online after he told me he was a surgeon but it drew another blank. I'm done with the fishing expeditions.

"I like that it's uncomplicated," I admit. "There's no expectation about when he'll call. I never feel disappointed if he hasn't called in days. It's just easier if we keep numbers out of it."

"Easier?" she mocks my tone. "You just told me that you meet him at a coffee shop in the mornings. You only know sparse details about him. For all you know, his real name is Greg and he's a trapeze artist."

I'll take that to mean that she's fucked a man named Greg who likes to hang in the air.

"Aren't you the one who is always telling me that if something isn't broken it doesn't need to be fixed?" I take a tentative bite of the apple she gave me when she walked into my apartment. "What Evan and I have is not broken."

"It's not broken," she agrees quickly. "It's just really fucked up."

"Why does fucked up have to be a bad thing?" I ask with a laugh. "If I like him and he likes me, I don't see any reason to change anything between us."

"You're heading down a slippery slope at breakneck speed." She wraps the apple core in a paper napkin. "This is going to end with you hurt. I feel it and it breaks my heart."

"That's not going to happen." I wave away her comment with a brush of my hand against her knee. "Sooner or later it will run its course and we'll both walk away with no baggage and absolutely zero regret."

***

Evan pins his eyes on me. "Can you even talk? I thought I cheered loudly but you're something else. I'm surprised you haven't lost your voice."

I push against his side with my elbow. "It's a proven technique to help with player motivation. Don't tell me that you've never heard of it."

He stops to pull me close to him. We're on the sidewalk outside the café. We ran into each other here more than twelve hours ago when he told me that he had tickets to tonight's game. He apologized for the short notice, but I was excited.

I met him back here after I went home from work to change into jeans and a white sweater.

We laughed when we took off our coats in the hockey arena and realized that he'd chosen a white sweater and jeans too.

"You're beautiful." His lips skim over mine. "How can a person be so beautiful inside and out?"

The words catch my breath just as much as the kiss does. It's romantic and unexpected. It's also near midnight and as much as I'd like to find a room so we can spend the next few hours together, I don't want our perfect second date to end in an uncomfortable bed in an hourly rate hotel.

"Come home with me, Chloe."

I almost lose my footing when I hear those words. It's an invitation I wasn't expecting and now, I'm unsure whether I should accept or not. This is unchartered territory for the two of us. I repeat the question back to be certain that I heard it correctly. "You want me to go home with you?"

He kisses me. It's tender and filled with desire. "I want you in my bed. I want to smell you on my sheets. I want you to see where I am when I'm dreaming about you."

Do I want that too? I think I do.

I know I can trust him. He didn't have to tell me about the broken condom but he did. He could have fucked off and avoided me for eternity. That's not hard to do in this city.

"I'll go home with you," I say against his lips. "I can't wait to go home with you."

Chapter 27

Evan

There are times when I readily admit that my dick gets the best of me. That's not what happened tonight. I want Chloe to see where I live. I need her to understand that I value her and I can't convey that if I keep taking her to cheap motels for sex.

I can't do that anymore. I knew before I met her at the Roasting Point Café that I'd ask her back here.

My heart skips a beat when we walk through the door and into the apartment. I know it's not a palace by any means. She doesn't strike me as the type to judge.

"It's cold." She tugs her coat tighter around her. "Did you leave a window open?"

I huff out a laugh. "I turned the heat down when I left."

She nods as she watches me cross the room to adjust it. "I do that too sometimes. I figure why should I heat an empty space? It makes no sense, right?"

How the fuck is she so perfect for me?

"I'd rather use the savings to buy you a dozen pink roses." I point out a bouquet sitting atop my kitchen table. I put them in a large beer glass that I cleaned up and filled with water. "I was hoping you'd say yes when I asked you to come here."

Her gaze volleys between the roses and my face. "Those are for me?"

I nod. "I tracked your brother down at his gym one morning. It's fucked up. I know it is but I needed to know what flowers you liked."

She moves to the table and bends down to smell the roses. "These are beautiful. I can't believe you had them here waiting for me. You knew I'd come home with you, didn't you?"

"I hoped." I stalk toward her. "I'll never assume anything with you, Chloe. I like that you're unpredictable."

She gifts me with a small smile. "You think I'm unpredictable?"

Our eyes meet and hold for a beat. It feels like time stops. "I think you're incredible."

"I think that about you too." She narrows the space between us with a few short steps. "I like your apartment, Dr. Evan."

"I love that you're standing in it."

She perches on her tiptoes to give me a soft kiss. "Take me to your bed."

***

His big body hovers over me as he fucks me with long, leisurely strokes.

We've been in his bed for hours. I took him in my mouth before he was even able to get completely undressed. He didn't come. He stopped me by pulling me up to my feet and pushing me onto the dark sheets.

That's when he removed my clothing, piece-by-piece. It was torturous when he rained kisses over my skin. He moaned through words of appreciation for the shape of my breasts and my hips.

I begged him to fuck me because I was so wet from his touch and those words.

When he sheathed himself and entered me, it felt like my chest caved in. There was a burst of something unfamiliar. It might have been fondness or more, but it was everything in that second.

"I could stare at you like this for hours." He ups the tempo and my body responds instantly with a circle of my hips up toward him.

"I wouldn't complain if you did," I whisper back as I watch the way his lips part slightly with each thrust of his cock inside of me.

He throws his head back with a deep growl. "I feel like you were made just for me. Our bodies are so perfect for each other. God, it's so fucking good."

I can't speak. I'm nearing the edge. I can feel my body heating and my pulse racing.

My eyes close and I listen to his breathing. Heavy breaths laced with the subtle nuance of a grunt. It's raw and animalistic.

I cry out when the orgasm hits me. I say his name because I want him to know that he's the reason I feel so much. He's the man who has helped me heal and made me trust.

He ruts into me with steady, even strokes as I come around his cock.

"My turn," he whispers against my neck. "I need it hard tonight, Chloe."

I nod as my pussy clenches around him.

A noise breaks through our labored breaths. I stall him with two hands on his biceps. "Evan."

"Fuck." He pumps two more strokes before he pulls back and settles on his knees between my legs. "My phone. I have to get it. Shit, I'm sorry. I'm so sorry."

I feel bereft but I don't say anything as he pushes himself to his feet and grabs his jeans from the floor. He fishes in the pocket for his phone and with his back to me he answers in a tone that's barely more than a whisper.

"This is Dr. Scott. What is it?"

Chapter 28

Evan

When I turn back around after the call, Chloe is already on her feet. I move toward her. I know she heard my name but why the fuck would I care about that? I just had the best sex of my life in my own bed.

She knows where I live. I don't see any reason not to tell her my surname.

"Do you need to go?" She bends down to pick up her panties. "I'll get dressed."

I push both of my hands through my hair. "We have time. I don't need to leave yet. The patient is being monitored."

She doesn't stop what she's doing. Once the panties are on, she finds her bra. "I should still go. It's late and I have a lot to do tomorrow."

"It's Saturday," I point out as I adjust the bra strap on her shoulder. "Your boss doesn't force you to work weekends, does he or is it she?"

She sighs. "I work for myself. It's a small practice. I'm building it up slowly."

This woman is a force of nature. It's impressive. It's damn impressive that she's betting everything on herself.

"Can I use the washroom?" She shifts from one foot to another. "That soda I had at the arena is catching up with me."

I laugh softly. "It's across the hall."

She starts toward my bedroom door but before she's halfway there she drops to both knees.

"I feel so…" Her left arm moves behind her in search of me.

I'm there. I drop to my knees too and pull her next to me. "What's wrong? Tell me what it is?"

"I'm so dizzy." She rests her head against my chest. "I feel really dizzy."

"I need you to try and stand up." I inch up to one knee. "Lean on me. Just lean your entire body weight on me and I'll take care of you."

She nods without any hesitation before she slowly gets to her feet. "I didn't have much to eat today."

"Your blood sugar is low." I help her back to the bed. "Sit here and I'll get some juice. Promise me you won't try and stand."

Her eyes meet mine and I know she instantly sees all the concern I feel for her. "I'll wait right here for you."

I jog to the kitchen and fill a glass with orange juice. I'm back next to her in less than two minutes.

"Drink this." I push the glass toward her. "Drink it all."

She nods as she brings it to her mouth and takes a large swallow. "I haven't been that dizzy in years. I think the last time was during chemo."

Time stops. I'm pretty fucking sure my heart does too.

Chemo?

I look down at the floor because you can't say that word to me and not expect me to press for more. It goes beyond the fact that I'm a fucking doctor. I know the brutality of those treatments. I watched someone I love try to fight her way to the other side in one piece.

"What brand of orange juice is this?" she asks after she takes the last sip. "I like it."

I can't fucking remember. How the hell would I remember that? I buy the cheap stuff and shove it into my fridge so I can down a glass between shifts.

I want to ask about the chemo but that moment has passed. I'm not even sure she realizes that she let the word slip.

"Do you need to go be a surgeon now?" She hands me back the empty glass. "I think I'll be fine now."

"I'll take you home on my way."

She's saved by the bell. Literally. My phone starts ringing again.

Fuck that thing.

I pick it up from where I tossed it on the bed. "What is it?"

I hang my head as I listen to Kylie rattle off a series of numbers that should be making sense to me. I can't focus. All I can think about is the fact that Chloe had chemo at some point in her life.

"I'm leaving now," I say brusquely before I end the call.

"I'll be fine to get home on my own." Chloe stands and puts her hands on her hips. "I'm good as new."

I look at her face. Jesus. All I want is to tuck her in my bed and keep her there. This woman has been through way too much in her life already.

My phone starts up again. I want to smash it against the wall but I can't. I fucking can't because I need to get to work so I can assist Kylie in surgery.

"I'll get dressed and find my way home." Chloe leans forward and kisses my cheek. "Thank you for everything, Evan."

Thank you for storming into my life. I ache to say the words but I don't. Instead I answer my phone and watch her get dressed before she walks away.

Chapter 29

Chloe

"Can food poisoning last a week?" I take a seat on a bench in Central Park. "I was queasy again today."

"You look a little green." Gabi tugs on the end of my hair. "Maybe it is the flu. It's prime flu season. Don't breathe on me."

I can't help but laugh. "There are other symptoms with the flu. It's not just nausea."

"You said you almost passed out at Evan's apartment last week." She juts her index finger in the air. "That's another symptom. If I were a doctor, I'd diagnose it as the flu."

"You're not a doctor," I point out the obvious. "Maybe I need to go see mine."

"I get worried." She reaches for my hand and gives it a tight squeeze. "I always get worried when you're feeling under the weather."

I do too but this is not anything serious. I know my body. I've been in remission for years. "It's nothing to be worried about, Gabi."

"Promise me you'll make an appointment with Dr. Reynolds to get checked out."

I did miss my yearly physical so it wouldn't hurt to have a check-up. "I'll make the appointment as soon as we're back at the office."

She shoves her phone into my hand. "Do it now, Chloe. She may have an opening today."

***

I scratch the back of my neck while I wait for Dr. Reynolds in her office. When I called for an appointment, the receptionist told me that they had a cancellation at the end of the day. I was tempted to pass on it since I felt so tired today, but I knew that Gabi would steal the phone from me and agree to the appointment herself.

I twirl a piece of my hair around my finger. I have a feeling that she's going to tell me to eat three square meals a day and work out. I strive for the first, but the second is where I falter.

Going to the gym doesn't fit into my schedule. I don't have the time to devote to it right now and if she pushes, I'll tell her that I'll stroll around Central Park on my lunch break.

I turn in the chair I'm sitting in when I hear the door to her office click shut. The sound is innocent but it washes over me like a tidal wave of memories.

I spent too much time in doctors' offices and hospitals when I was sick. I hated every minute of it and even though I know I have to have regular check-ups, I don't rush to make them.

"Do I have the flu?" I ask as Dr. Sadie Reynolds rounds her desk. She's older than I am by a few years. Her long brown hair is braided to the side and her blue eyes are trained on the tablet in her hands. "My assistant is convinced that I have the flu."

"It's not the flu," she says with little emotion. "It's not that at all."

I wait until she's sitting behind her desk before I ask the next obvious question. "It is something though?"

She nods silently.

My stomach clenches in disbelief. I feel fine. I may have been nauseous on a couple of occasions and I had that near fainting spell at Evan's apartment, but none of that was serious enough to warrant the concerned look on her face.

She knows my entire medical history. She's a general practitioner but she's taken the time to understand all of my medical challenges to date.

"What is it?"

She closes the tablet and places it on her desk. "Chloe, I'm a firm believer in miracles."

I feel tears in the corners of my eyes. This can't be happening. I can't be sick again. I have a life now and a future.

"How bad is it?" I whisper the words as I drop my head. "Just tell me how bad it is."

"Some people will tell you that the terrible twos are the worst, but my son is inching toward being a pre-teen and the attitude can spin my head around."

I look up and into her face. She's smiling. Why is she smiling?

"I'm sorry about your son but I don't understand what that has to do with me."

She rests her hands in the center of her desk and swallows hard. "You're pregnant, Chloe. You're going to have a baby."

Chapter 30

Evan

I spot her sitting at a corner table when I walk into the Roasting Point Café. This is the first morning I've been able to pull myself away from the hospital in days. It's been almost two weeks since I've seen Chloe.

I'm mildly surprised that she hasn't shown up on my doorstep again. I half-expected her to and it's possible that she has. I'm rarely home and since there's no doorman, I have no idea if she's been around or not.

As much as I'm craving a cup of coffee, I don't stop to order one. I'm too anxious to see Chloe. I want to touch her and kiss her.

Most of all, I just want to hold her hand and gaze into those gorgeous hazel eyes.

She looks up as I approach and I can sense that something is wrong immediately. She's bundled up tightly in a wool coat even though temperatures are spring like today. Her eyes are sullen and dark. I can tell that she was crying at some point this morning.

"Chloe," I whisper her name under my breath as I reach for her.

She doesn't stand. Instead she leans toward me and squeezes my hand briefly before she drops it.

I don't question what that's about. Instead, I take a seat next to her, tugging the wooden chair across the tile floor until our knees are touching.

"Tell me what's wrong?" I ask immediately as I circle my hand around her shoulder.

She looks into my eyes before her gaze drops again. "I don't know how this happened."

"What happened?"

"I can do this. I know I can and I want to. I really want to but I'm so scared."

I skim my fingers over her cheek to catch a tear. "You can tell me what's going on, Chloe. I want to help you but I can't do that if I don't know what's wrong."

"I don't need you to help." She reaches for my hand to cup it against her cheek. "I hope that you'll want to but if you don't I'm okay on my own. I have a good job and my apartment isn't big but it's nice enough."

I try to tangle all those pieces of information together into something that makes sense. "I'm not following you. Can you slow down and start from the beginning?"

"I can." She nods her head. "I can start from the beginning."

That's something. I take both of her hands in mine and kiss them. "I'm here for as long as you need me. Start at the beginning and take all the time you need."

She hiccups through a soft sob as her eyes lock with mine. "I went to the doctor a few days ago."

I try to keep my hands steady. "Are you still feeling faint?"

"It was only that one time at your place." She bites her bottom lip. "My friend, Gabi, insisted I go because of my medical history."

"Your medical history?" I ask with a cocked brow.

"I was very sick when I was a teenager." She sighs heavily.

"Cancer?" I question as my stomach knots.

"Leukemia. Chronic myeloid leukemia. I don't know if you know what that is."

I swallow hard. "I know."

"I'm in remission but the chemo it did things to my body."

It ate it from the inside out. I know. I don't need her to tell me what it can do to a person. I've seen it firsthand.

"Evan." She turns to face me. "I need you to know something."

I kiss her softly as I rest my forehead against hers. "Tell me."

"If I thought there was any chance, I would have told you." Her eyes close. "I would have taken precautions, but I thought it was impossible."

"You thought what was impossible?"

Her eyes open and it hits me. It fucking hits me before she says another word. "I'm pregnant. I don't know how it happened but you and I are having a baby."

***

I want to bolt. There's a part of me that is tempted to head straight for the door and leave this in my past. I can't go through this again if it's going to end the way it did last time.

My work is my family now. I love caring for people and every form of comfort I need I can get in the corridors of the hospital when I'm doing my job.

"I'm terrified," Chloe says softly. "I never thought this would happen to me."

If I were a dick and she were any other woman, I'd push her to clarify what exactly her fertility specialist told her. I don't do that because I know she's as genuinely shocked by this news as I am.

"I always wanted to have a baby," she goes on as she picks at a corner of the table with her fingernail. "I gave up on that dream when my husband left me."

Asshole.

The man has to be insane to leave a woman like this behind.

"Life is funny," I offer in a hushed tone. "You never know when it's about to throw you a curve ball."

A smile blooms on her lips. "This feels like more than a curve ball."

It is. I feel like my entire world has been turned on its axis. "We should talk about what we'll do."

Her hand reaches for mine. "I meant it when I said I can do this on my own. I have my family to help and my friend, Gabi. I make good money. I can fit all the baby stuff I need in the extra bedroom of my apartment."

There's no way in hell that she just learned about the pregnancy today. She's been sitting on this information for at least a day or two. "When did you find out, Chloe? When did you see the doctor?"

She circles her thumb over my palm. "Two days ago. I came by here yesterday morning but I couldn't find you. I wanted to tell you."

"Give me your number." I tug my hand free and reach into the front pocket of my jeans to grab my phone. "I need it, Chloe. You're having my baby."

She calls out a series of numbers and I type them into my phone before I send her a quick text.

Her eyes drop to her phone's screen. "Is that your number?"

I give her a curt nod. "Enter it into your contact list. I want you to use it whenever you need to."

I type her name into my contact list along with her number before I put my phone back on the table.

"We will talk about all of this, right?" She tilts her head to look at me. "You'll think about if you want to be a part of the baby's life, because you can tell me it's not for you and I'll get it."

She's too nice for her own good. "I'm not going anywhere, Chloe. This baby is as much mine as it is yours. We will figure out the logistics and get everything in place before its born."

Her expression shifts slightly. "Thank you for not freaking out. I did enough of that for us both."

She has no idea how hard my heart is hammering inside my chest right now. I'm still trying to absorb the news. A baby. My baby. I'm going to be a dad.

"I need to get to my office." She moves to stand. "I'll be in touch soon, Evan."

I stop her before she can walk away. "I still want to see you, Chloe. I know this is a lot and it complicates everything, but I hope we can see each other again."

A beat passes before she says anything. "I'd like that. Call me sometime for a date. I might say yes."

Chapter 31

Chloe

Evan is the only person I've told about the baby.

I've never been pregnant but I know that the risk of a miscarriage is highest in the first trimester. I don't want to get too attached to the idea that I'm going to be a mom. It might not happen.

I'm still coming to terms with the news that I'm pregnant. I tried for so many years and with each disappointment I fell deeper into a pit of depression.

"Ms. Newell, we'd be thrilled if you'd join in on this discussion." The mediator looks to where I'm sitting next to my client. "I've asked your client the same question four times and since you seem oblivious to her voice, I thought I'd attempt to reach you."

I look at the woman sitting next to me. Margo Chance hired me to represent her after she lost her job at a retail store. She spent much of the past twenty years selling shoes to Manhattan's elite and when the owner decided to expand to an online presence, her job as a sales clerk was cut.

Fortunately for her, she signed an employment contract that guaranteed a sizable pension upon retirement. It's my job to negotiate the terms of her severance and secure as much of that pension as I can for her.

"What was the question?"

The mediator shuffles the papers in front of her around on the table in a lame attempt to intimidate me. This isn't the first time that I've dealt with her and I know all of her tricks.

"Ms. Chance is prepared to take a smaller severance in exchange for her full pension." I don't wait for the mediator to pull the question out of the blue. "Anything else is unacceptable to us and the terms of her employment contract back up our position."

The mediator looks to the lawyer representing the store when he starts to speak. "Chloe, we're not changing our stance on this. She'll get six weeks of pay and we'll graciously allow her the benefit of twenty-five percent of her pension."

"And you wonder why I was ignoring you, Norman," I volley back to my not so esteemed colleague. "She's been a loyal employee for decades. Her sales kept the business afloat through a string of lean years. Give her what she deserves. You don't want her to fill in her retirement income with a job at your competitor, do you? There's nothing in her contract about trade secrets. You can quote me on that."

He slams the file folder in front of him closed. "Fine. We'll sign off on what she wants, but it comes with the stipulation that she retires as of today."

Since she's nearing seventy-years-old and is eyeing a condo on Florida's sunny coast, it fits right into her schedule. "Agreed, Norman."

With that the meeting is adjourned and I'm free to head back to my office to think about the fact

that I may be holding my baby a little over seven
months from now.

***

I spot Evan instantly when I walk into the near
empty restaurant. It's almost eight p.m. and I was
already at home in my sweatpants and a T-shirt
preparing notes for my court date tomorrow.

He said he needed to talk to me and since he
had an opening in his schedule, I put on a bra under
my T-shirt, traded my sweatpants for jeans and took
the subway to this place.

"I'm glad you came." He stands as I approach
him.

I've never seen him in scrubs before. They're
light blue and even though he's wearing a black
hoodie over the top, it's obvious that he left work and
came directly here.

His arms circle me in a tender embrace as his
lips skim my forehead. "You look good. I can tell
you're more rested than you were the last time we
saw each other."

I am. I still wake up in a panic at least a few
times each night but I'm coming to terms with the
fact that I'm going to be a mom.

"You look good too," I offer, not just because
it's polite but it's true.

He's gorgeous and now that I know that I'm
having his baby I can't help but hope that it will have
his blue eyes and smile.

"Is everything okay?" I ask as I take a seat.

When he called his voice was low and his tone serious. He didn't go into details about why he wanted to see me but I instinctively knew that it wasn't for a hook-up. Judging by the serious expression on his face, I'm right.

"How are you feeling?"

I shrug off my sweater and sigh. "Good. I still have mild nausea in the morning but the dizzy spells have passed. I'm more tired than I usually am but Dr. Reynolds says that's to be expected."

"Sadie?"

I lock eyes with him. He knows my doctor. She works out of an office on the Upper East Side but does see patients at one of the hospitals too.

"Your doctor is Sadie Reynolds?"

I nod. "She's been my primary care physician for a few years. She's the best."

"She is." He smiles broadly. "I'm glad you're in such good hands."

I let out a sigh. "She told me at my appointment yesterday that I'll need to see an obstetrician soon. She's putting together a list of recommendations for me but she said some may not be available."

"Rita Bergstein is the best in the city." He waves the server who is approaching us away. "I can make the arrangements for you to see her."

It's a kind gesture and would take a load of worry off my shoulders. "I'd like that."

"I'll make the call first thing tomorrow morning."

The persistent server approaches again. "Can I get you anything?"

I glance at the almost empty plate of pasta in front of Evan. It's obvious that he had a meal before I arrived. I took this as a dinner invitation even though I ate a salad and a piece of salmon at Gabi's place earlier.

"I'll have a cup of herbal tea," I say quietly.

Evan doesn't respond so the server takes off in the direction of the kitchen.

"I don't know how to bring this up." He nervously taps his foot against the tiled floor. "I know it's early and we haven't discussed in detail how this arrangement will work."

"This arrangement?" I question with a raised brow.

"I want to be there for you and the baby, Chloe." He blows out an exasperated breath. "I'll help you with any medical costs and I'll make sure that the baby is taken care of."

I'm grateful for that. I earn a good living but I didn't realize how much stuff I'll need to welcome my newborn home. I started adding it all up yesterday and I had to close the calculator app on my phone because of anxiety.

"I appreciate that." I swallow hard. "But it's so early. We don't have to get into all of that yet. I haven't even gotten through the first trimester yet."

"My lawyer says it's never too early to get a plan in place."

"You have a lawyer?"

He nods. "He's technically a friend. He practices family law so I thought I'd check in with him. I don't know the first thing about two people who just met having a baby together."

His words sting. We may not know each other very well, but I've started to feel a strong connection with him. I thought the feeling was mutual but apparently I misread that.

"Look, Chloe." He moves to touch my hand but pulls back before he makes contact. "Forgive me for this but it's a subject we need to address. Griffin, my lawyer, brought it up and it's been gnawing at me."

I look up as the server approaches and places the tea on the table in front of me. "Thank you."

Evan waits until he's out of earshot before he drops a bombshell in my lap. "Once you are eight weeks along, I'm going to need you to take a paternity test. I can't get invested in this if the baby isn't mine."

Chapter 32

Evan

I don't know why the fuck I don't trust my gut in situations like this. When I called my friend, Griffin Kent, to talk to him about how I could legally help Chloe, he immediately mentioned the idea of a paternity test.

I laughed at first because Chloe doesn't strike me as the type to fuck more than one guy at a time. I told Griffin as much but he brought up the fact that even if she only slept with me since that night, she may have been with someone else in the days leading up to our one-night stand.

Pushing that possibility aside was easy when I was at work. It was the moments between when I was alone in my apartment or on the subway that doubt crept in.

Now, I'm sitting across from her and the expression on her face erases any questions I have. She looks stunned and hurt, even if she's trying to put on a brave front.

"Of course," she answers as she picks up the small china teacup. "I haven't been with anyone else in a long time, but you'd be remiss if you didn't ask for a paternity test. As you said, we don't know each other very well."

Fuck. I fucked up.

I didn't have to bring this up today. I could have waited until she was at least in her second trimester. She's been through so much shit in her life and when she's finally in reach of one of her dreams, I smash it under my heel with the inference that she sleeps around.

"Let's put that aside for now," I try to retreat and save the conversation.

"No." She puts the teacup back down without taking a sip. "It's a valid point. I'll ask my doctor about when a test like that can happen."

I'm frustrated with myself. I didn't have to bring this up tonight but my past edged me on. One bad experience can taint a person forever.

"I'll call Rita tomorrow and we can set up an appointment that works for us both."

"Why?" She leans back in her chair. "I have insurance. I'll go to the appointment and report back to you. If it makes you more comfortable, I'll give Dr. Bergstein permission to share the details with you herself."

"I want to be there for you, Chloe."

She pushes to stand. "I'm a big girl. I can handle a doctor's appointment. Besides, you're always busy. You don't have to take time away from your work to hold my hand."

I stand too, unsure of what to say next.

"Let's put the help on hold until you can be sure that your investment in this is valid."

"My heart tells me the baby is mine, Chloe."

Her hand drops to the T-shirt that's covering her flat stomach. "It is, Evan. You'll see and once you do, we can work out the details of what works best for the baby because that's the only thing that matters to me."

It's not the only thing that matters to me. She does too and I'm scared that I've fucked up the best thing that's ever happened to me.

***

"You haven't been your usual insulting self, Evan." Jordan pats me on the back. "What's up?"

I look over my shoulder at him. He's been beaming ever since Kylie and him decided to go exclusive. There isn't a soul who works in this hospital who saw that one coming. They are about as mismatched as two people can be, but obviously there's something there. Kylie looked just as happy this morning when I saw her after my rounds.

"Your ear hair is longer than the hair around my dick." I arch a brow. "Does that make you feel all warm and fuzzy inside?"

His hand leaps to his ear. "My barber usually takes care of that. I'll have to ask Kylie to trim them tonight."

I turn back to face the x-rays in front of me. "Sounds like a fun date. Maybe she can take on your toenails too."

"How do you know about my toenails? My podiatrist said that cream he gave me would help."

I huff out a laugh. "That's both disgusting and fascinating."

"Fascinating how?"

He moves so he's standing next to me. Other doctors are milling about but we've all learned to mind our own business unless asked. It works well for us. You have to be as focused as you can be when you're dealing with life and death cases on a daily basis.

"What does Kylie see in you beyond the obvious?" I circle my finger in front of his face.

He skims his hand over his cleanly-shaven chin. "I listen to her. I appreciate her. I make her feel special."

I'm not buying it. "What else?"

He lowers his voice. "The sex is phenomenal."

"Phenomenal?" I ask as I study the x-ray. "Your word or is that coming from Kylie?"

"I had a dry spell before I met her," he admits. "There was a lot of pent up energy waiting to be released. Kylie was the beneficiary of that."

I turn my attention to the tablet in my hands as I make notes on the x-ray and the treatment plan I'll discuss with the patient this afternoon. "If you make each other happy, I'm all for it. I have to admit, I didn't think it would progress into anything."

"No one did." He chuckles. "We're an unlikely pair, but when there's a connection that's undeniable, you've got to go for it. That's what I did and look at me now."

I do. He looks relaxed and content. I can't use either of those words to describe myself at the moment.

"Keep her happy." I poke him in the shoulder. "Or I'll come for you. I'm an expert with a scalpel. Don't forget that."

"That's why I'm here." He opens the cover on his tablet. "I need you to consult on a case. I'm on the fence on this one and I want you to push me over to one side."

I take his tablet and run through the information on the patient's chart. "Send this to me and I'll have a closer look this afternoon."

"You and I make a great team, Evan." He gives me another pat on the back. "As much as I like, Kylie, you're the best vascular surgeon we have."

It's a compliment I never thought I'd hear. It means a lot. "Thank you, Jordan, I appreciate that."

"You didn't let me finish." He grins as he reaches to take his tablet back. "You're the best vascular surgeon we have without ear hair. You'll never be as good as me."

"I'll take second best over that ear hair any day of the week." I grimace. "Seriously, man, get control of that before you trip over it."

Chapter 33

Chloe

"So you'll be able to do the paternity test without having to get near the baby?" I rub my stomach. There's still nothing there to speak of other than a small roll that I've been trying to work away with sit-ups for the past six months.

"We can do it with a simple blood test once you pass the eight week mark." Dr. Bergstein glances at the calendar hanging on the wall in the exam room. "You're going to hit that milestone soon, Chloe, so you can talk to the baby's father and arrange for him to call in so we can set up a time for him to have his blood drawn. We'll require a sample from you too."

Since her office is across the street from one of Manhattan's busiest hospitals, I have to wonder whether Evan is close.

"Evan Scott said that you two know each other," I say because maybe she'll put two-and-two together and realize that my potential baby daddy is her friend.

"Evan Scott?" she repeats back with a furrow of her brow. "Oh, yes. We met years ago. He's a great guy. I take it you two are friends too?"

Technically, we aren't friends at all. We're two people who are having a baby together.

"I know him, " I admit because I don't know how to classify what we are.

She turns her attention to a prescription pad in her hands. "I'm going to give you a prescription for pre-natal vitamins. You should take one daily."

"I can do that." I scoot forward on the exam table. "I'm good to go?"

"You are." She looks over at me. "If you see Evan anytime soon, tell him I said hi and that I hope his little guy isn't running him ragged."

There's no way in hell that's a euphemism for Evan's penis. It's not a little guy. I need clarification because I only have sparse details about the man I'm about to share a lifelong connection with in the form of a living, breathing human being. "His little guy?"

She moves toward the closed door. "His son. Kim switched doctors before the birth but I was there the day they found out it was a boy. I don't think I've ever seen a happier man than Evan that day."

I slide off the table and pick up my purse before I take the prescription from her. I follow her out into the corridor and as she leads me back to the reception area her words ring over and over in my head.

Evan is already a dad.

That's a surprise I didn't see coming.

***

Dealing with everything that's been thrown at me lately on my own was a good plan until I realized just how overwhelmed I am.

After I saw Dr. Bergstein I went to the pharmacy and dropped off my prescription. I listened as the pharmacist explained the benefits of the vitamins to the baby. She had kind eyes and when she asked if I had any questions, I almost blurted out that I needed advice about how to talk to my baby's dad about his son.

I didn't because it would have obviously been highly inappropriate and also because there's someone else who will give me the advice I need.

He's sitting across from me now.

"When you invited yourself over I didn't think it was so we could have a staring contest, but I'm game, Chloe. You know I can beat you any day of the week."

I laugh. "I didn't come here to stare at you."

Rocco looks around his modest apartment. "Was it for the ambiance? As you can see none of that exists here."

I dip my chin down. I called him on my way home from work. I told him that I had something important to discuss with him and by the time I stepped into his building, I was already filled with doubt.

"I need someone to talk to, Rocco."

That draws him to his feet and over to where I'm sitting on a leather sofa. He takes a seat next to me. "I'm here. You know I'm always here."

He's the same age as Evan but they couldn't be more different. Rocco lives his life day-by-day, exploring new adventures whenever they present themselves. He travels on a whim and sometimes leaves New York for weeks at a time.

Evan's life is confined to a hospital where he devotes himself to bettering others.

"I wish my mom was still here," I say through a sob. "I love you, but I just wish she was here."

"Me too," he confesses as he circles an arm around my shoulder. "I loved her too. I miss her every day."

I know that he does.

All three of my brothers wept at my mother's funeral service. They'd come to love her as much as I did. When she died, our lives were upended but we held fast to each other.

Our love for her and for each other kept us afloat.

"I'm here, Chloe. Tell me what's happening."

I inhale a sharp breath as I look at his kind and compassionate face. "I'm pregnant."

Chapter 34

Chloe

"Pregnant?" Rocco's gaze drops to my stomach before it skims over my face. "Chloe, are you sure? You and Chris tried for so long. How is this possible?"

Christopher Newell and I tried for years to start a family. He's older than I am by two decades and very successful. I met him when I interned at his law firm before college. He divorced his second wife, pursued me and I finally gave in.

Our wedding was everything I thought I wanted. It was the perfect life on the outside, but behind the doors of our apartment on Park Avenue, it was an ongoing battle to have a child. Christopher wanted an heir and I couldn't deliver, so I became his third ex-wife.

"My doctor said that miracles happen." I manage a small smile. "I've always had irregular periods and the fertility doctors that I saw with Chris told me that the chemo had damaged my eggs. No one thought this was possible, Rocco, yet it's happening."

He tugs me into his chest. "It is a miracle. You're having a baby. What did dad say? He must be over the moon."

I push back so I can look up and into his face. "I haven't told anyone. You're the only one who knows."

"Did you tell Evan?" he questions. "I don't want to jump to conclusions but I've seen the way the guy looks at you. I'm assuming he's the dad."

"He is…" I trail off not sure of how to tell him that Evan isn't quite as sure as I am and he already has one child to take care of.

"What's the problem? I don't know him at all, but I don't see you getting involved with a deadbeat. Is he not going to step up to the plate and own this?"

I watch as his jaw ticks. Rocco is a master at covering his emotions but when he's angry, there's little he can do to veil that.

"We're going to do a paternity test." I pat his knee. "That's part of this process."

"Why do it if you're both sure he's the father?"

It's a valid question that I don't have an answer to so I resort to asking him a question of my own. "If you had a one-night stand and the woman got pregnant, you'd want a paternity test, wouldn't you?"

"Hell, yes," he says empathetically. "We're not talking about a one-night stand, Chloe. We are talking about two people in a relationship."

I'm not surprised that he has blinders on when it comes to my personal life. "Evan and I started as a one-night stand. We both believe that's when the baby was conceived."

"I understand, " he finally says after staring at me for a beat. "The details don't matter. What matters is that you're going to be a mom and you've got your family to lean on."

"Thank you." I kiss his cheek. "There's something else that I want to talk about."

His eyes widen. "I can't imagine it's going to be more mind-blowing than what you just told me, but I'm all ears."

"I found out that Evan has a son." I hear the tremor in my voice. It's the first time I've said it aloud, even though I've been replaying Dr. Bergstein's words in my mind all day. "He didn't tell me. I heard about it from someone else."

He leans his back against the sofa. "How well do you know this guy, Chloe? A kid seems like a pretty big deal to me. You'd think he'd want to share the good news before you two got too serious."

This is the part of the conversation that I've been dreading. "Do you know how I told you it was casual? Well, it's really casual. We only exchanged numbers after we found out I'm pregnant."

"It's not casual anymore. You two are going to share a child. If you heard he already has one, you need to talk to him about that. It's going to impact your baby's life since they'll have an instant sibling."

"You're right." I nod my head in agreement. "The next time I see Evan I'll ask him about his son."

I will. I just need to use the time between now and then to figure out how exactly I'll do that.

***

I feel my cheeks blush as Evan approaches me. He's dressed in a black suit with a white dress shirt underneath. He's carrying a bouquet of pink roses in his hand.

I'm not dressed nearly as smartly as he is. I'm still wearing the plain black dress I've had on all day. Meeting him for dinner was his idea and since I had a late meeting, I agreed that seven p.m. at the pasta place was the best I could do.

"You look very handsome," I say as he stops in front of where I'm standing just inside the door.

The place is busier than the first time I met him here.

He pushes the bouquet at me. "You're radiant, Chloe. I don't know how you can be more beautiful each time I see you, but you are."

I like that he thinks so. I know he's not just saying it. He believes it.

I follow him and when he pulls out a chair next to a table, I sit. "I'm glad you called me. I've been wanting to talk to you."

"You can call me whenever you want." He takes a seat next to me. "If I'm busy it will go straight to voicemail but I'll call you back as soon as I can."

I take comfort in that. Once he realizes that he is indeed the father of my child, I'll need him more. I have no idea what it's like to go through a pregnancy and then the early days of the child's life. Evan does. He's already tackled it all once.

"I'll remember that." I place the roses next to me on the table. "Dr. Bergstein said we could do the paternity test once I'm eight weeks along."

"I know I'm the father." He places both his hands on the table. "I don't know why I doubted it. It might have been fear. I've been through this before, Chloe."

"I know," I admit. "I heard about that."

My words take him aback. He runs a hand through his hair. "You know about that? There's no way you can know about that, Chloe."

"Dr. Bergstein let it slip." I shrug. "I admit I was surprised but I know now. I think we have to discuss how it will impact both of them."

He looks right at me, his eyes trained to mine. I see confusion mixed with frustration. "What exactly did Rita let slip?"

"I know you already have a child, Evan," I say evenly. "I think it's great. Our baby will have a sibling from the start and I couldn't be happier about that."

Chapter 35

Evan

Rita Bergstein has no idea what the fuck she's talking about.

"I don't have a child, Chloe." I point at her. "This baby will be my first child."

"Are you sure?"

I laugh because I'd know if there was a child of mine out there. At least, I hope I'd know. I keep my dick wrapped up during sex for a reason.

"I don't have any children," I continue, because I want her to understand that Rita wasn't pulling random facts about me out of the air. "About five years ago a woman I spent a night with told me she was pregnant."

She starts to say something but her mouth slams shut before one word escapes.

I get it. She's thinking about herself. We spent more than one together but she ended up knocked up because the condom failed during our first night together.

"Her name was Kim." I hate that fucking name because the woman who owned it put me through hell. "We fucked one time and a month later she tracked me down at the club we met at to tell me that I was going to be a dad."

Silence is all that greets me, so I go on, because I want Chloe to understand that she's nothing like Kim and our situation won't end the way that did.

"I believed her." I rake both hands through my hair. "I didn't question it because she gave me a song and dance about not having time for sex, so I was the only lover she'd had that year."

Chloe's brows rise. "You said you met in a club?"

"I know." I sigh. "How many celibate people hang out in clubs? I get that I was an idiot for believing her. I was at a low point in my life at that time and needed something. I wanted something to give me hope and that baby was it."

"I understand." She pauses, "I think I understand."

Vague understanding is enough for me at this point. I go on, "I went to every doctor's appointment with her. She saw Rita before she switched to another OBGYN. We moved in together and the day the baby was born was the happiest of my life."

"What happened after that?"

My chest tightens. "I had doubts right away that he was mine and when I ran into her ex-boyfriend leaving the hospital room the day after she delivered, I knew. The cocky grin on his face told me everything."

"I'm sorry, Evan."

"Don't be." I brush her words away with a wave of my hand in the air. "I told her I wanted a paternity test, she cried. I persisted and it proved that her baby wasn't mine."

She blinks at me. "That must have been hard."

"It was fucked up," I manage a small laugh. "It made me realize that I wanted a baby at some point but it also made me run out and buy seven boxes of condoms that night."

"It's good to be prepared." She raises both hands. "I should have been. If I knew there was any chance that I could get pregnant, I would have been on the pill or whatever else women use to stop that from happening."

"It was fate, Chloe." I reach across the table to take her hands in mine. "That or I have super sperm."

She throws her head back and laughs. "I think it was a combination of both. Whatever it was, you and I are having a baby."

***

"It's okay to do this while I'm pregnant?" She looks over her shoulder at where I'm standing behind her. "It's not going to hurt the baby will it?"

I love that she's so concerned about our child. "It's very safe, Chloe. I'm a doctor so you know that you can trust me."

She dips her head back down to the blanket. "I bet you've used that same line on thousands of women."

I slide my cock into her wet and warm pussy. I ate her out when we got to my apartment. I extended the invitation after we had dinner. I needed her here. I've been craving her like mad and I could tell that she wanted the same thing when she rested her hand on my thigh in the cab.

I wrapped my dick but I was tempted to ask if I could go bare. I'm clean. I know she has to be. "Your pussy is so tight. Fuck, it's like a glove."

She rocks her hips back and forth, gliding her wetness over me. I stand still so she can control it all.

Her breathing increases when she arches her back and takes me deeper. "I love this. God, I love this."

"I love it too," I rush the words out as I dig my fingers into the soft flesh of her hips. "Use me, Chloe. Make yourself come on my cock."

She does. She speeds up the tempo, and then slows and when my finger finds her clit, she flies over the edge and the feeling, that fucking feeling, of her coming around my dick is enough to make me shoot my load.

Chapter 36

Evan

"My mom died two years ago." Her warm breath traces a path over my neck.

I don't move because it's a confession that came out of nowhere. After a quick recharge of juice and a shared apple, we fucked a second time. After that, both spent we fell asleep in each other's arms.

It's too late for her to go. I don't want her to. That's why I've wrapped myself around her. I need her here, with me, while I sort through the fucked up shit that my heart is starting to feel.

"I'm sorry," I whisper with my lips against her forehead. "Do you want to talk about it?"

She nods. "It was sudden. She was on her way to my apartment when she collapsed."

Guilt. She may have moved past it by now, but the fact that she added the detail about where her mom was headed when she died, tells me more than the words do.

She waits for a beat before she speaks again. "She was always there for me. Always and when she needed me, I wasn't there to help her."

I should offer words of comfort about how no one can predict what will happen on any given day, but in my line of work, I know that little helps when someone is lost forever. "I can't imagine the pain you and your brothers were in."

"My dad too." She runs the tip of her finger over my chest. "He loved my mom with everything he had. I tried to be strong for him, but I fell apart."

I pull her closer, wanting to negate any distance between us so she feels every part of me. I need her to know that I want to swallow her pain. I long to steal it from her. I want to protect her from any more of life's bullshit.

"I wish she was here to meet the baby." She nuzzles closer. "My mom would have been an incredible grandma. I just hope that I can be half as good of a mom as she was."

"I think you'll make a great mom," I say softly. "You'll be an amazing mom."

She murmurs something I can't make out before her breathing evens. I hold her while she sleeps and when I start to drift I pray that this pregnancy goes smoothly so she doesn't have to face another heartache.

***

I sit on the edge of the bed and watch Chloe sleep. She's content and comfortable and that's all I want her to feel forever.

We all have challenges and stories to tell. Chloe's are tragic but they haven't dampened her at all. She's bright and beautiful. There's a light in her eyes that tells you that she sees promise right around the next corner.

Despite everything she's been through, she's not jaded.

I wish I could say the same for myself.

I've wandered through life with a chip on my shoulder. I've spent too much time pissed off at the world for what it's taken.

I glance at the clock on the table next to the bed. It's past midnight here.

My phone hasn't made a sound since I met up with Chloe and I'm grateful for that.

I'll check in at the hospital before I crawl back into bed, but first, I need to make a call to California.

My sister, Carmen, didn't make it through her battle with leukemia the way Chloe did. She suffered a stroke and her life is a shadow of what it used to be.

She doesn't let it stop her though. She's a teacher, a wife and one day soon she'll be an aunt.

I scoop up my suit jacket and tug out my phone so I can call her and tell her the good news. It may be premature but it'll give her some hope in a world that's still filled with too much disappointment and pain.

I dial her number as I stand and walk out of my bedroom.

She answers instantly. "Evan?"

"I'm having a baby, Carmen," I whisper so I don't wake Chloe. "I'm having a baby with the most incredible woman I've ever met."

Chapter 37

Chloe

I should have probably told Evan last night that I overheard him talking to someone about me. He thought I was asleep but I woke when I felt him shift on the bed to reach for his phone.

He told the person he was speaking to that he's having a baby with the most incredible woman he's ever known. I rolled over and shut my eyes again, overcome with raw emotion.

After he crawled back into bed, we snuggled together under the covers before I fell back asleep. I didn't wake until this morning when I felt his lips touching mine.

Our goodbye wasn't awkward at all and when I got back to my apartment to shower and get ready for my day, I ran my hand over my stomach.

I'm still scared and unsure of what's going to happen when the baby arrives, but the feeling of pure terror has been replaced with mild fear.

"Why are you staring at that crib?" Gabi steps in place next to me.

I've spent the past twenty minutes waiting for her on 5th Avenue. We went out for lunch today and on our way back to the office, she decided that she needed a new tube of mascara.

Since I don't have another client meeting until three, I told her I'd tag along. I could only stomach a few minutes inside the Matiz Cosmetics store before I had to make a quick exit back to the street.

The Matiz fragrance line is lovely but it didn't agree with me today. Then scents were so strong that I felt faint. I thought I'd wait outside the store until I spotted the quaint boutique next door. The window display is of a nursery complete with a beautiful white crib.

It's simple, elegant and filled with an array of stuffed animals.

This is my future. It's what I've always wanted; yet every time I think about the day the baby will arrive, I feel a rush of anxiety.

When I was struggling to conceive during my marriage it was with the comfort of knowing that I had a stable life. I had a loving partner by my side. We lived in an apartment with enough room for four children and money wasn't an object.

My life couldn't be more different now.

I'm still dealing with the fallout from my messy divorce, I'm having a baby with a man I just met and I live in an apartment that won't leave much extra room after I equip it for a newborn.

I shake off thoughts of what my future looks like and focus on Gabi.

"It looks like you picked up a lot more than one mascara." I point at the Matiz shopping bag in her hand. "That should last you a year."

"They had a few essentials on sale." She beams. "I cannot pass up a bargain on my beauty products. I'm all stocked up so I won't have to come back for at least a few weeks."

I don't want the subject of why I was gazing longingly at a crib to come up again, so I morph into boss mode. "You've stretched your one hour lunch break to two-and-a-half. I need to get you back to the office so you can earn some money to pay for all of that."

"I'm counting on the raise you're going to give me next month." She steps toward the curb to wave down an approaching taxi.

I stand in stunned silence. We went through the same thing last winter. Gabi asked for a raise, I told her to wait until summer and then she pestered me continuously until I caved and gave her the salary bump she deserved.

"I'm not going to win this wage war, am I?" I move to where a taxi has now stopped for us. "Be gentle with your demands, Gabi. I may need a little extra money for myself this year."

"I'll be kind." She lets me slide into the backseat of the taxi first before she gets in and slams the door behind us. "I'll be sure to leave you at least a little for yourself."

***

"I got us this ginger tea for our celebratory toast." Evan fumbles with the tea bag in his hand. "Champagne would have been my first choice, but I didn't want to torture you by drinking it in front of you."

"I can handle this." As I reach forward to take the tea bag, our hands brush against each other. "I'm an expert with these things, Dr."

He inches closer to me as I pour hot water from the kettle into both of the ceramic mugs on his counter.

"You smell amazing, Chloe." He runs the tip of his nose over the sensitive skin of my neck. "I hope our baby smells as good as you."

I shiver as I turn to look into his eyes.

Today was the day. We both received an envelope delivered via courier with the paternity test results.

Evan called me when his arrived and asked if I'd had a chance to open mine. I hadn't because I already knew what the results would be. I tucked it into my purse and told him that I'd drop by his place after we were both done work.

I was on my way home by six, but Evan couldn't get away from the hospital until ten so now we're at his place, enjoying a warm cup of ginger tea.

"Where's your envelope?" he asks me as I hand him a cup.

I nod toward a chair next to the kitchen table. I had dropped my coat and my purse there after he let me in. "It's in my purse. I put it in there after it was delivered today."

He reaches into the back pocket of his jeans to pull out a folded envelope. "This is mine."

I look down at it expecting that it would be torn open but it's not. It's sealed shut, just like the one in my purse. "You didn't open it?"

"No." He places it down on the counter. "I know what the results are going to be. I'm the baby's dad. I feel it, Chloe."

That brings tears to the corners of my eyes. I wipe them away with a swipe of my hand. "My emotions are all over the place lately. One minute I'm sad, the next I'm mad. I feel sorry for my assistant."

He places both his hands on my hips. "Emotions are good. You need to get them all out. I do. My colleagues would tell you that I'm a bastard one day and a prince the next."

"It's hard to imagine you acting like a bastard." I reach up to cup my hands around the back of his neck. "I've only ever seen the charming side of you."

He lowers his lips to mine. "You bring out the best in me."

Chapter 38

Evan

"We don't have to fuck every time we see each other, Chloe." I'm even stunned when I hear those words leave my lips.

Chloe looks just as shocked as I feel. "I was taking off my sweater because it's warm in here, Evan. I have a T-shirt on underneath. Did you think I was just going to strip here in the kitchen so you could bend me over the table and have your way with me?"

I slide my hand over the front of my jeans. "Now you've gone and made my cock hard."

Her gaze travels down my body. "I'll take care of that later. You said that you know what the results of the paternity test are, but are you going to open it?"

I look over at the envelope. When it was delivered to the hospital earlier I was in surgery. Vanessa was the one who handed it to me afterwards.

She didn't ask me what it was about and I didn't offer. I trust her, but I'm not going to share the news about the baby with anyone at work at this point.

I have every intention of introducing Chloe to Jordan and Kylie very soon. I want her to meet Jack too.

Although we haven't had a discussion about where our relationship is headed other than to a delivery room, I want the people in my inner circle to know the woman I'm falling for. It just so happens that she's also the mother of my child.

Sometimes fate smiles down on you twice.

"I don't need to open it." I push it aside. "I trust you, Chloe. If I can't trust you what future do we have together?"

The teacup in her hand wobbles. "Our future? You mean like when the baby comes and we see each other when you're passing her off to me and I'm bringing her over here for your days?"

There's way too fucking much to absorb in that response. I hone in on the part about the baby's gender "You think it's a girl?"

I've had dreams of being a dad to a little girl. It's not that I've ever longed to be a father other than that stint I served as Kim's pseudo-baby daddy. Sometimes when I'm dead tired from working myself into a coma, I'll dream about holding a small girl and I instinctively know that it's my daughter.

"I want a healthy baby." She rubs her hands over her stomach. "I'll be happy either way."

"But you said *her*, Chloe," I point out as I cover her hands with my own. "Do you think we're having a little girl?"

She gazes down at where our fingers are linked together. "I feel that, but maybe that's wishful thinking? I'd love to have a son too. I'd teach him all about hockey."

"If it's a girl, you'll teach her all about hockey too," I say softly as I rest my cheek against her head. "This baby is going to be just like you. It's going to be fearless and strong. It'll storm over every challenge in its way."

She leans into me. "I know we haven't talked about it and it is way in the future, but I want you to be there when the baby is born, Evan. I want you next to me watching our child come into the world."

I swallow back a rush of emotions. I want that too. I want to be there for the delivery and every moment after but those are discussions for another time. I can't ask this woman to give me a future. She just vaguely mentioned what it will be like when we have a custody agreement in place and we meet to hand off our child to each other.

"I'll be there." I kiss her forehead. "I'll always be there for you and the baby."

***

She's hot. Sweat is peppering the back of her neck and her shoulder blades. I push against her, my arm wrapped around her, my fingers working furiously to get her off.

She moves with precision, keeping the pressure just where she wants it. Her clit is swollen and ripe. I circle it slowly knowing that it's driving her mad.

"I can't wait to feel you inside of me." Her voice is tempered with need and raw desire. "You're clean. I know you are."

My cock hardens even more. I haven't asked for a bare fuck but I'll take if she's offering. I've never felt the sensation before of a woman's warm wet pussy surrounding my hot flesh.

I pull her leg over my thigh so she's open. She adjusts her hips, pushing back against me. I run my fingers over the fleshy cheek of her ass. I grip it, kneading the softness in my fist before I slide my hand to my cock.

I bring it to her pussy, and glide it along the smooth silken skin.

She tries to push back onto my dick, but I want to savor this. I want to implant every sensation in my mind.

"Don't rush," I tell her with my lips to her ear. "Take it slow."

She whimpers but slows her pace. She lets me take over and I use the tip of my dick on her clit. I circle it pressing hard enough to give her what she wants but tender enough that it only prolongs the sweet, painful agony for me.

Her body squirms against me as she nears her release. The sheets are fisted in her hands, her legs moving in tandem with the waves of pleasure coursing through her. I sense when she's near the edge and my desire takes hold.

One hard thrust and I'm inside of her. I curse when I feel her come around me. The sensation like nothing I've ever experienced before. I grab her hips and pump, even strokes while she rides the high of one orgasm into another.

I twist her body until I'm on top of her from behind and with an arm under her stomach to prop her up, I fuck. It's hard, relentless and when I come inside of her and feel the release, I collapse; exhausted from head-to-toe and aching with a need that only this woman can satisfy.

Chapter 39

Chloe

I stare down at the screen of my phone.

I read the text message again and again. It's unexpected and unwelcome. It's also breaking the rules of the agreement that was signed just six months ago.

Call me, Chloe.

If it was anyone other than Christopher Newell, I would call, but the man has made my life hell for the past two years since he threw me out of our apartment and tried to steal most of my belongings along with my dignity.

Our divorce was complicated and tumultuous. He wanted out of the prenuptial agreement I signed when I was just nineteen.

My parents were captivated by his charm and wealth. They encouraged me to sign on the dotted line without a lawyer's approval.

Rocco wasn't as trusting. If it weren't for him, I would have left the marriage penniless and despondent. He paid for a consultation with one of Manhattan's premier family law experts and the agreement I finally did sign, gave my marriage a price tag if it ever ended.

The problem was that Christopher knew there were loopholes including a clause about me being unfaithful.

I never was.

He was the only man I was with.

I lost my virginity to him and he stole ten years as a bonus.

"Do you have a naked picture of Evan on your phone?" Gabi strolls into my office.

"What?" My head snaps up. "What did you say about a naked picture of Evan?"

She gestures toward my phone. "You're staring at that thing. You never do that. You skim your messages, answer emails quickly and then you put it down. You're not as attached to your phone as I am to mine."

I place my phone on the desk hoping that the text message from my ex-husband is just a mirage and when I check back it will be gone.

"Do you need something, Gabi?"

"A hard cock and a stiff drink." She shakes her head. "I am wound up tight today."

I blink my eyes. "It's only noon. I can't imagine what you're going to be like by the end of the day."

She plops down into one of the chairs in front of my desk. "My mom is driving me crazy. She wants to come to New York for a weekend. An entire weekend, Chloe. That's two full days of my life that I'll have to give up for her."

I'd give up years of my life for an extra hour with my mom to tell her that I love her and to thank her for every moment she devoted to me while she was alive.

"How do I get out of this? I saw her at Christmas. I don't need another dose this soon."

"You're selfish," I say quietly, hanging my head to hide my tear filled eyes. "You're so lucky."

She's silent for a moment before she finally speaks. "I'm sorry. I didn't think, Chloe."

I look up and she's perched on the edge of the chair, her hands fisted together in her lap.

"I need my mom right now more than anything." I wipe my hand over my face to brush away the tears. "I'm scared of what's about to happen to me and the only person in the world who could make me feel like everything will be okay is my mom and she's gone."

"Chloe." She's on her feet and around the desk in an instant. "What do you mean? What's about to happen to you?"

I can't meet her gaze so I look over at the window and the light snow that is falling. "I miss her, Gabi. She'd tell me it was all going to be okay and I'd believe her."

"I'll tell you the same thing." She crouches next to my chair. "Whatever it is you're going to face it. You're the strongest person I've ever known. I can help too if you tell me what it is."

I shake my head as a hiccup through a sob. "I can't."

"Ever since you went to see Dr. Reynolds, something hasn't been right." Her voice quivers. "You've been tired and quiet. We barely hang out. I'm scared, Chloe. I'm so scared that I'm going to lose you."

I look at her and see the tears in her own eyes. I can't do this to her. Gabi crawled into my hospital bed more times than I can count when I was sick. She brought all my schoolwork to the hospital and read my favorite books to me. I can't put her through this.

"Tell me, Chloe." She rests her forehead against my arm. "Please tell me you're going to be okay."

I stroke the back of her head while I whisper the words, "I'm pregnant, Gabi. I'm going to be a mom."

When she looks up and our eyes meet I don't see fear, but joy. "You're fucking kidding, right? This is not April Fool's Day."

I laugh through a stream of tears. "It's not a joke. I got knocked up the first time I slept with Evan."

She cradles my cheeks in her palms. "You're happy, right? This is a good thing, isn't it?"

I nod. "It's a very good thing."

She kisses my cheek before she stands. "You're going to slay this mom thing, Chloe and if you need any help, me and my mom will be there for you every step of the way. I'm going to run and call her back. You'll have lunch with us when she comes to visit, right?"

"Right," I answer softly. "I'd love to see your mom again."

Chapter 40

Evan

The early morning meetings at Roasting Point Café have ground to a halt. That's not by design. It's by necessity.

Work has been brutal. I've been pulling long shifts and taking on surgeries that I'd normally assist in with Kylie. She's out with the flu and although the other surgeons are doing their part to pick up the slack, the brunt of the overflow has fallen square on my shoulders.

Normally I wouldn't mind.

This is where I thrive. The rush in helping other people pushed me into this career in the first place.

I didn't follow in anyone's footsteps. My parents are both plastic surgeons. Their faces and bodies are their billboards. The private practice they run in Beverly Hills keeps them close to my sister and closer yet to the celebrity clientele that they adore.

I moved across the country for college so I could choose a specialty that I wanted. The fact that I'll never take over their practice is another nail in their coffin of disappointment.

By some miracle, maybe my son or my daughter will find worth in helping others find their inner beauty on the outside.

"How are you feeling, Mr. Peterson?" I tack a smile onto the end of that because Wilford Peterson looks like he could use it.

"Screw you."

"You'll have to wait at least six weeks until you engage in intimate activities, Mr. Peterson, and unfortunately for you I'm seeing someone."

The corner of his lip darts up before it falls. "I feel like shit."

"You look like hell." I point out as I circle the pen in my hand in front of his face. "Your color will improve in a day or two. I take no responsibility for your attitude."

"You're a smart ass. Do you know that?"

"I graduated at the top of my class. "I tuck the pen back in my pocket before I adjust the drip on his IV. "I'm going to prescribe something stronger for the pain and for the sake of the nurses. It'll knock you out for a few hours."

"Do you have a wife?" He looks down at my left hand.

I sigh. "No wife."

"Mine isn't here." He shrugs which is followed by a wince. "I thought she'd be here when I woke up."

"She fell asleep in the family lounge an hour ago." I point at a room across the hall from where we are. "She's a strong woman. You're a lucky man."

"You gave me a few more years with her, didn't you?" His wrinkled brow furrows. "She needs me. I can't leave her yet."

"I opened the clogged artery, stuck a shiny new stent in there and gave you more time with your beautiful bride. "

"There's little better in life than a woman who loves you." He fists the thin blue blanket that is covering him. "I'm grateful that you took care of my heart so I can take care of hers."

I hear words of gratitude from my patients and their families on a daily basis. I've never grown tired of it, but when it becomes a regular part of your day, numbness sets in and it takes a conversation like this to kick you in the ass and make you appreciate life.

"I'll wake her on my way out." I pat his hand. "I'll be back to see you this afternoon. Until then, keep the insults to a minimum. You're no match for the nurses on this ward."

He finally smiles. "I'll be good to them. You be good to yourself and keep your hands off my wife. You're more her type than I am."

I laugh as I stroll out of the recovery room. "Deal, Wilf. You've got yourself a deal."

***

I watch Chloe eat a sandwich. It's pastrami on rye with extra mustard and a dill pickle on the side.

"Do you have any strange cravings yet?"

She stops mid chew to look at me. Her brows pop up before she answers once she swallows. "Nothing like that. I just eat what I normally would."

"You'd normally down an entire bowl of soup and a sandwich at lunch?" I gesture to the empty bowl in front of her. "I had the soup too. It wasn't good."

She looks over at my half eaten bowl of chicken noodle soup. "You don't appreciate the subtle nuances of the broth."

"I don't appreciate that this came out of a can and they're charging us eight dollars a bowl."

"Today is my treat." She pats her purse. "You always pay for food. I want to pay today."

I shake my head as I yank my wallet out of the back pocket of my pants. "I'm not letting you pay, Chloe. This meal is on me."

"I can pay half." She starts to open her purse and her phone chimes from within. "I have to see who that is. I have a few major cases on the go."

"I love when you talk like a lawyer."

A laugh bubbles from her. "If that's the case I have a few things for you to think about."

I inch forward so I'm closer to her. This diner is crowded but since we're sitting in a corner booth, we're tucked away from most of the other patrons who are most likely doing the very same thing we are and that's having a quick lunch in the middle of the day.

"Tell me, Chloe. Talk lawyer to me."

She leans in until her breath is skating over my lips. "Constructive discharge. Front pay and I can't stop thinking about overtime compensation."

"I'm hard as nails."

Her hand slides under the table and lands on my thigh. "You're not, are you?"

I kiss her softly as I cover her hand with mine and inch it toward the front of my pants. "I am and it has nothing to do with what you just said and everything to do with wanting to fuck you."

She skims her fingers over the ridge of my cock. That only heightens my desire more.

The sound of a phone ringing breaks the moment. I instinctively reach down to tug mine from my pocket but Chloe has her phone out and on the table before I reach mine.

A scowl forms on her face when she sees the incoming number.

"Leave me the hell alone," she says under her breath. "Just stop."

"Who is it?" I arch my neck to see the screen but her hand moves to cover it.

"No one." She presses the ignore button. "It's no one I ever want to talk to again."

Chapter 41

Chloe

I seethe with anger as I sit next to Evan. My jerk of an ex-husband ruined a perfectly hot moment between the man I'm falling for and me.

Evan has no idea who was calling me. For all he knows it was a telemarketer. I didn't bother to tell him that it was the asshole that broke my heart. I'm over Christopher and I never want to talk to him again.

"We can talk about it, Chloe."

I look at him. The playfulness that was in his blue eyes a minute ago has been replaced with concern. I hate that. I despise the fact that a simple phone call from my ex can impact anything between Evan and I.

"Or we sit here and I can watch you shake in anger." He scratches his top lip. "I'm good either way for the next twenty minutes and then I need to get back to work."

I glance down at my watch. The hour we had planned together has flown by. I was excited when he texted me this morning to suggest lunch. I've missed seeing him at the café in the mornings and even though we talk and text multiple times a day, it's not the same as being near him.

"What kind of surgeon are you?" I ask as I slide my phone back into my purse. Ignoring Christopher has worked all week, so I'll keep up that tactic until I'm forced to change it. "I've been meaning to ask for weeks but I always think of something more important to talk about and that gets pushed aside."

He laughs. "Something more important? Give me an example of something that you thought was more important than that question?"

"Our baby," I answer with a small smile. "We're doing the whole relationship thing upside down. You realize that, don't you?"

"Upside down?" He looks amused. "Clarify that for me."

"It's pretty obvious." I roll my eyes. "You and I had sex and I got pregnant before our first date. Most couples have a few dates, get to know each other, fall in love and then start thinking about a baby."

He looks at my face for a few seconds before he responds. "Do you consider us a couple, Chloe?"

I can't tell if it's a legitimate question or not. We've never talked about what's developing between us. I know he feels something. I see it when we're together in the way he looks at me and in the tenderness of his touch.

I'm uncomfortable answering so I take the tried-and-true approach that any good attorney would. I toss the question right back at him. "Do you?"

I wait for him to press for me to answer first, but that's not what happens.

"I do," he says as his eyes search mine. "I consider us a couple."

My heart flutters and even though the baby is tiny, I'm sure it can feel my joy. "I do too."

He kisses me with his incredible mouth. His lips are soft, his breath sweet and when he breaks the kiss and looks into my eyes, I see the future that I've always wanted reflecting back at me.

***

I round the corner to my office after having lunch with Evan and stop dead in my tracks.

Christopher Newell is not supposed to be standing on the sidewalk in front of my office building. We agreed that I'd stay the hell away from him if he would do the same. Apparently, the man hasn't changed at all. He couldn't keep up his end of the bargain when he promised to love me forever either.

Physically, he looks just as he did the day he kicked me out of our apartment. He's tall and thin. His dark hair is still peppered with just the right amount of gray thanks to his stylist's expert touch.

He's clean-shaven and dressed in a suit that costs more than some people's yearly salary. Smugness surrounds him like a cloud of dust.

I draw in a deep breath and stalk toward him. I won't back down. Whatever it is that he wants, I'll deal with it now.

"What do you want?" I ask as I near him. He spins on his heel to face me. "Chloe, dear, there you are."

Dear? It was one of the many endearments he used when we were together. I used to covet those pet names until I realized that they were tools in his emotional arsenal. He knew how to control me with romance and the promise of a future.

"What do you want?" I repeat, not giving him the satisfaction of a response to his words.

He eyes me from head-to-toe. I'm grateful that I'm wearing a long coat. I can't stand the thought of any part of him touching me, not even his gaze. "You'll be sad to know that Bertram passed last week."

That does sadden me. Bertram Phillips was Christopher's driver for years, which meant he was mine as well. He was older, kind and impossibly hard not to love. He was one of the shining lights in my life after my mother passed. "How?"

"Heart attack." Chris rests his palm against his chest. "In his sleep. God rest his soul."

I push past him to get to the door. "You didn't have to come all this way to tell me. A call to my attorney would have sufficed."

His hand leaps to my shoulder to stop me. "I needed to tell you in person. Bertram left you something. A bequest in his will."

I look up and into his face. I feel nothing. The butterflies that were there when he first locked eyes with me at his office more than a decade ago have long flown away. I don't have the yearning desire to kiss him anymore. All I see when I look up at him is an insecure man who valued the future much more than the present.

"Bertram left me something?" I shake off his hand as I step back. "What is it?"

His hand dips into the inner pocket of his suit jacket. He pulls out a silver fountain pen and hands it to me. "He put a note in his will that you'd understand."

Tears sting my eyes as I reach for it. "I do understand. I do."

Chapter 42

Evan

For someone who is pregnant and wearing heels, Chloe can walk faster than most people in sneakers.

We said goodbye at the diner and as she walked away, my phone rang. It was Jordan with a rundown of an update of one of my patients. I cut him off with the promise that I'd be at the hospital in ten minutes but that plan hit a snag when I realized that Chloe had left her scarf on the bench next to the table.

I could have tucked it in my pocket until the next time I saw her.

It would have been easy to call or text her to tell her that I had it, but I chased after her instead.

She had a good half block on me before I was stopped by a light. By the times I caught up to her she was stopped on a sidewalk talking to a man. He's older, distinguished and from what I can make out, he looks a hell of a lot like someone I've met.

I stand silently near the corner watching as she takes something from his hand before she turns and walks into an office building.

He shakes his head before his hands rake through his dark hair.

When he starts walking in my direction, I approach him. I rarely forget a face and his has become imprinted in my brain because of one conversation we had years ago.

I wait until he's just about to pass me by before I call out to him. "Hey. I know you don't I?"

He turns then and I see no recognition in his eyes. "I don't think so."

I push because I'm sure this is the same guy that I sat next to in the hospital chapel. "I'm Dr. Evan Scott. You're Chris, right? I swear we met at the hospital a couple of years ago. I was in the chapel and you sat down…"

"Next to you," he interrupts me. "What the hell are you doing in this neighborhood?"

What the hell were you doing talking to Chloe?

I glance down the block to see if Chloe has exited the building but she's not there. "I'm visiting a friend. Do you work around here?"

His gaze darts to the street next to us. "I work uptown. I'm waiting for my driver to circle the block to pick me up. He's new and apparently slow as fuck."

Arrogance. I have it and use it wisely. This guy doesn't wear it well at all.

"That night at the hospital," I begin trying to find the right words. "I remember you had a lot on your mind. Did it all work out?"

He glances back over his shoulder to where he was standing with Chloe not more than three minutes ago. "You could say that. I took your advice and I didn't look back until now."

"You took my advice?" I question as I watch a black town car slow to a stop on the street next to us.

He moves toward it. "I divorced my wife. She couldn't give me what I wanted so I ended it that night. I had her things packed up before she got home from the hospital."

"Your wife was at the hospital too?"

He nods as the driver rounds the car to open the back door. "My wife's mother died that night. I was in the chapel praying to God that he'd give me a sign to leave Chloe. You asked if I needed anything and when you told me to think about what would make me happy, I knew that leaving her was the only choice I had."

What the fuck?

"Your wife is named Chloe?"

He lowers himself into the backseat, smoothing his suit jacket with his hand. "Chloe Newell, although she's dropping that to go back to her maiden name. It's career suicide but she's never been bright."

My hand fists.

"I just saw her." He sighs deeply. "I'd still fuck her brains out but knowing that she'll never give me a son makes it a waste of my time."

The driver slams the car door shut and I try and resist the urge to open it back up, haul him out of the and make him feel every ounce of pain he's caused Chloe.

***

"I need you to check on something for me, Jordan." I approach him from behind.

"What?" He doesn't turn to face me and it pisses me off. That's not on him. I'm still mad as fuck at Chris Newell and myself for sitting next to him at the hospital chapel two years ago.

My mind has been reeling since he drove away. I didn't go into the building that I saw Chloe enter. I couldn't. I'm the fucked up reason her husband left her. He goddamn left her the night her mother died.

I need the big picture before I can go to her and confess that I'm the guy who told her husband to look out for himself and leave her.

The conversation I had with him has always stayed with me.

He was alone in the chapel when I walked in. I sat next to him because he looked like he could use a shoulder and I needed one.

Solace can be found in the walls of that place with strangers.

I've sought counsel there on many times and I've offered advice to the families of patients who are either praying for a miracle or trying to accept the unthinkable.

When he started talking about life, death and regret I listened. He said his wife couldn't give him what he needed and it was tearing him apart. He hated her for it and the resentment that had started as a drop had grown into an ocean.

I wasn't in a good place so I told him to do whatever the fuck made him happy. I told him that life was too short to waste it on relationships that weren't fulfilling.

He mentioned leaving his wife, I gave him my friend Griffin's name and number and he told me he'd call him that night to start the process of divorcing his wife.

Chloe. That was Chloe.

She was the woman who couldn't give him what he needed and I now know with certainty that he was talking about a child.

"I said what do you need?" Jordan spins around and looks right at me.

I ignore his freshly plucked brows because I don't have time to ask him what the fuck happened to his face. "I'm trying to find a patient. It was around two years ago. Her last name would have been Jones. She collapsed on a street. I need to know her cause of death. You know someone in records, right? You can give them that and they'll figure it out?"

He holds my gaze. "I don't need to go to records. I was there when she died. You were too."

Tension tightens my shoulders. There's no fucking way. "I wasn't there."

"She was brought in after collapsing on a sidewalk," Jordan begins.

"You're not thinking of the woman with the abdominal aortic aneurysm?" I interrupt.

"That's her." He rests his hand on my shoulder. "Irena Jones, aged fifty-five. I'll never forget that one. She coded on the table right after we opened her up. We were too late, Evan. She died right in front of us."

She did. I remember everything about that night. The piercing sound of the monitor as her pulse stopped; the wails from the waiting room when Jordan went to tell her family that she was gone. I'll never forget the sight of a woman with her head buried in the chest of her father while she wept for the mother that she'd never see again.

I caused all of that. I was the man who changed Chloe's life forever that night and fuck if I know how I'm going to tell her.

Chapter 43

Chloe

I slam the desk of my drawer before I rest my face in my palms. "Dammit. Just dammit."

"That's not the greeting I was hoping for but I'll take it."

My head pops up to see Rocco standing in the doorway of my office with a basket of fruit in his hands.

"Is that for me?" I tilt my head. "I hope it is because I'm starving."

He strolls in and places it in the middle of my desk. "I have no fucking idea what a pregnant woman likes so I picked a few of everything and shoved it in there for you."

I blow him a kiss. "You're the best. I haven't been eating enough fruit and now I don't have an excuse."

He sits on the edge of my desk and scoops an apple from the basket. "What had you upset when I walked in?"

I skim my fingers over my neck. "I lost my favorite scarf. I can't remember where I left it."

He fingers the light gray one wrapped around his neck. "You're welcome to take mine. I'm heading down to Boston for a few days and it's windy as hell there. I can do without for you."

I pat him on the thigh. "You keep that one for yourself. It's too masculine for me."

He sets the apple back down before he picks up the silver fountain pen that Christopher gave me. "This is beautiful, Chloe. Where did this come from?"

I reach to take it from him. "Do you remember Bertram? He used to drive me and Chris everywhere."

His jaw tightens at the mention of my ex-husband. "I do remember him. Did he give that to you?"

I slide my fingers up and down the pen. "He left it to me. He died last week."

"Shit." He shakes his head. "That's too bad. He seemed like a nice guy."

I look up at my brother. If anyone can be labeled a nice guy it's him. "He was always there for me. He came to see me a few times after my mom died."

"That was good of him but why do you think he left you a pen? Does it have any significance to you?"

I slide it onto my desk and squeeze my eyes shut briefly. "Bertram came to get me the day I signed my divorce papers. He said it would have pissed Chris off but that's why he did it."

Rocco laughs. "I wish I would have known this guy."

I smile as I continue, "I didn't ask him to go up to the office with me, but he did and when it was time for me to go into the conference room to sign, he handed me the pen. He said his mother had given it to him when he left Scotland to come here. He told me it was filled with luck so I used it sign the papers and I gave it back to him afterward."

"Treasure that pen, Chloe." Rocco slides to his feet. "You got your freedom back the day you signed those papers and look at your life now. Your dreams are coming true."

I gaze down at the pen. "My future does look pretty fucking bright, doesn't it?"

"You know it. Nothing is standing in the way of the life you've always wanted."

***

I dial Evan's cell number again and inwardly curse when it goes to voicemail. I can't exactly be mad at the man. He's busy at work and in his world that means helping people in a much more significant way than I do.

I cross the street after exiting the subway and make my way down the tree-lined sidewalk. The green buds of spring are starting to pop up. The cold winter wind has been replaced with a spring breeze.

I approach my dad's house with excitement. I've been waiting to have this conversation with him for weeks and I thought the best way to do that would be to show up out of the blue with a box of his favorite cookies from the bakery he used to visit all the time when he lived in Manhattan.

I'm just about to knock when the door swings open.

I stand in shocked silence when I see my dad in an embrace with a redhead.

"Chloe?" He scrambles to back away from the woman when he locks eyes with me. "What in the world are you doing here?"

The redhead spins around to face me.

She's my dad's age with soft creases around her green eyes. Her smile is warm and infectious. "You must be Chloe. I'm April."

I take her outstretched hand in mine and give it a soft shake. I manage to say a few words even though I feel as though my voice is caught somewhere between my stomach and my throat. "It's nice to meet you."

"April lives up the block." My dad's hand floats past my head toward the sidewalk. "We were having a coffee and…"

"Sharing stories," April finishes for him. "Your dad is a great storyteller, Chloe. I know all about you and your three brothers."

My mouth curves. "I hope I didn't interrupt."

"I was on my way home." April steps past me as she pulls her thin sweater around her shoulders to cover her purple dress. "If you two want a bite to eat later, I'll bring over some dinner. You just let me know."

I watch her walk away and when I turn back to look at my dad, I see something in his eyes that hasn't been there for a very long time. Hope.

I see no reason not to add to that, so I say the five words I've been holding inside for the past three-and-a-half months. "I'm having a baby, dad."

The hug he pulls me into tells me that we're both going to be just fine.

Chapter 44

Evan

I've been avoiding the woman I'm falling in love with for two days because I'm damn sure that everything between us will change when she realizes that I'm the guy who steamrolled her life into a million little pieces on a Thursday night two years ago.

I finally found what I was looking for online when I searched for Chloe Newell.

Image after image of my beautiful Chloe appeared. Some of them were from her days in law school but many were from her time spent as the head of an advocacy group for disabled workers.

She's put in her time to improve the community and she stood next to her dick of an ex-husband at a host of charity events to benefit others.

The pictures of Chloe standing alongside Christopher Newell made my stomach churn. She was obviously his trophy wife; a young woman meant to boost his ego and his stature among his friends.

I read a few interviews where Christopher stated that he was looking most forward to starting a family with Chloe.

It was all about the heir for him and when she couldn't produce it, he tossed her to the curb.

Their divorce has been dirty and filled with countless accusations all tossed at her. She's kept tight lipped about what tore her marriage apart, instead focusing on others who need her and building a career of her own.

When I tracked down a picture on a blog of their family on their wedding day, my worst fear was confirmed. The woman who had taken her last breath while I was readying to save her life was Chloe's mom.

The loss of a patient is never easy. Knowing that it was someone who Chloe cherished makes it almost too much to shoulder.

"You can't control what happened that night." Jack pushes his bottle of beer against my back. "You gave that ass advice not knowing that he was married to a great girl and you did what you could for her mom."

I watch as he rounds me before he takes a seat on my sofa.

"Are you going to pace the floor all night, Evan, or are you going to join me and watch the game?"

I can't sit. I can't think straight. I can't fucking focus on a hockey game.

"What if she blames me for everything?"

Jack glances over at me. "You didn't do a thing wrong. Why the hell are you beating yourself up about this? You saved her from a bad marriage and you tried to save her mother's life."

"I ruined her life in the space of two hours." I clench my fists at my side. "Her divorce has been a battle. She's been dragged through the mud and she's had to cope with her mom's death."

"All of that would have happened if you would have been at the hospital that night or not." He lifts his beer in the air. "It's not on you. None of this is on you."

I don't see it that way. "I'm the one who told her husband to dump her that night. I had no fucking clue that her mother had just died."

"He's the dick who made that decision."

"What if she never talks to me again?"

He raises a brow as he looks over at where I'm still standing. "You two are having a child, Evan. Even if she somehow blames you for that fucked up night, you're still going to co-parent this baby. Give her some credit."

"I know I need to talk to her about this."

"You need to find your balls and do it as soon as possible." He looks at the television. "If you keep this all a secret from her you'll regret it. Be honest. Tell her what happened and the two of you can put this behind you."

It sounds reasonable coming from him but he's not the one who changed the entire course of Chloe's life. I did that and before another day passes, I need to own that.

Chapter 45

Chloe

I look over at Evan when Dr. Bergstein's nurse calls out my name.

Chloe Newell.

He doesn't react which I suspect is because he did some digging and realized that I'm still lugging around my married name. I've been meaning to file the paperwork to change it back to Jones. I'm definitely doing that before the baby is born.

"Do you want the baby to have your last name?" I ask when we both stand to follow the nurse to the exam room. "Or we could do a hyphenated thing like Jones hyphen Scott or we could just name the baby Jones Scott."

He stops mid-step to look at me. "I want whatever you do, Chloe. Whatever makes you happiest."

I follow the nurse down the corridor with Evan next to me. "I'd like for its surname to be Scott. I want that for the baby."

A ghost of a smile slides over his mouth. "I'd like that."

We enter an exam room where Dr. Bergstein is already waiting. "I've got a full schedule and I'm actually on time for once. It's good to see you both. Evan, it's been awhile."

"Rita," he says quietly. "It's nice to see you looking so well."

"My nose is courtesy of your mother." She turns to show us her profile. "She does the best work. It's well worth the trip west."

He doesn't respond. I make a mental note to ask him what that was about once we're done.

"I'm going to do our regular exam and then we'll have a listen to the baby's heart."

I look at her face before my gaze slides to Evan. He looks as surprised as I do. "We get to hear our baby's heartbeat, Evan. I didn't know that was going to happen today."

He nervously shifts from one foot to another, his hand stroking his chin. "It's good. We'll hear it together."

I nod as I toss him a compassionate look. I know what he's feeling. He went through this once before and it turned out that baby wasn't his. I don't know if he's opened the envelope that contains the paternity test results yet, but I'm hoping that after hearing our baby's little heart beating, that he'll feel as connected to our child as I do.

"Hop up here, Chloe." Dr. Bergstein pats the top of the exam table. "We'll get started and we'll see just how strong the new little Scott is."

***

"Tell me why you're crying." Evan cradles me in his arms. "I want to help, Chloe. I need to know why you're crying."

The tears began as joy when we heart the whoosh and then the heartbeat of our beautiful baby.

It was steady and strong and Dr. Bergstein said it was a good sign of things to come.

We left her office and headed to Central Park. On our way there we passed a tourist bus and my tears morphed into something else.

My mom used to take me for rides on the buses when my brothers were too busy to hang out with us. My mom would pretend to be from out-of-town and would question the tour guide on every landmark we passed.

I lived for those moments when she'd make me laugh aloud.

We followed every single one of those rides with a hot dog in Central Park.

"I wish my mom could have been with us today." I look at a group of children playing on the grass. "When I was trying to have a baby years ago, she'd tell me that her greatest wish was to be a grandma. She never got it, and now that I'm pregnant, it's feels bittersweet."

He holds me close. "I wish she could have been here too. I would do anything in my power to change that day if I could."

It's a sweet thing to say. I would do anything I could too but the doctors tried valiantly to save her life. "No one could have done a thing."

"I could have," he insists. "I'm the best there is, Chloe."

I pull away so I can meet his eyes with mine. "I have no doubt that you're a wonderful surgeon, Evan, but you don't even know what was wrong with her."

He swallows hard. "Your mother died from an abdominal aortic aneurysm."

I stare at his lips. Did he really just say that? "I've never told you that."

His eyes close briefly before he locks them with mine. "I was there, Chloe. I was in the operating room. I was present when your mother died."

I'm on my feet in an instant, my hands pushing against the air around me trying to find room to breathe. "You weren't there. It was another doctor. You aren't him, Evan."

"Dr. Jordan Whitman made the notification to your family that night." He searches my face. "I'm sorry, Chloe. I wanted to save her. If I would have had more time, I might have had a chance, but it was too late."

"Too late?" I step back when he reaches for me. "You had a chance to save her life? You were there?"

"I was there," he says softly.

"You saw her die?" My voice cracks as my body shakes with a sob. "Did she suffer? Was she in pain?"

"No." He fists his hands at his sides. "It was quick. She wouldn't have felt anything after she collapsed on the sidewalk."

I turn away from him to sort through my thoughts. How could he have been there? I would have seen him. I would have felt something, wouldn't I? We didn't know each other then, but the bond that connects us now is so strong.

"There's more." I feel his hand on my shoulder. "I need to tell you something else."

I spin back around. "About my mom? Is it about my mom?"

"No." He hangs his head. "It's about your ex-husband. I'm the reason he left you that night."

Chapter 46

Evan

I'm grateful that Chloe decided we needed to take my confessional to a more private place.

She was shaking when we got in a cab near Central Park to go back to her apartment. I didn't expect that the first time I'd see her home would be the day I was dragging her heart through the dirt, but life doesn't always match up to my wants and needs and today is a prime example of that.

She didn't say one word on the ride here and I didn't either because what the fuck can a man say when he's just told the woman he loves that he was one of the doctors who attempted to save her mother's life and failed.

I step into the apartment after her. It's mid-afternoon and light is filling the space. The walls are painted light blue, the furnishings are white, the accessories mostly pieces of art and above the fireplace mantle is a framed picture of her family.

It had to have been taken years ago, since Chloe is wearing braces, but it perfectly captures the joy in the faces of all six people in the photograph.

I stare at her mother's face a moment longer than the rest. The regret of the day she died still haunting me.

Chloe drops her purse on the coffee table before she turns to face me. "How do you know Chris?"

"I don't." I shove my hands into the front pockets of my pants to resist the urge to hold her. "I met him the night your mother died. I went to the hospital chapel and he was there."

"So that's where he was?" She scoffs. "I looked everywhere for him after we got the news. I couldn't find him. I needed him and he was nowhere to be found."

I hate the bastard for not being next to her when Jordan delivered the news about her mother. I wish to fuck I would have been there for her. We were strangers then, but I would have felt compelled to take her in my arms. I know it. I feel it. The draw to be with her was strong from the first moment I saw her outside the hotel.

"I was reeling from the loss of your mother so I went to the chapel," I confess. "I always go there when a patient dies. I need the solace to collect my thoughts."

"We should sit." She moves toward a sofa and I follow. Once she's seated, I lower into the spot next to her. I want to wrap my arms around her but she's made no move to touch me. I'm trying to respect her needs even though I want nothing but to forget I ever talked to Christopher Newell that night.

My chest expands as I go on even though I feel like there's not enough air in my lungs. "Chris started talking about life and death and I listened. I needed to hear someone else's pain to help soothe my own."

I glance at her face and the look on it almost breaks my heart. I wait a beat for her to say anything but she's silent.

I clear my throat, desperate for a drink of anything to chase away what I'm feeling. "He talked about his marriage and how there was something missing. He said he needed more and his wife couldn't give it to him."

"So you told him to leave me?" Her voice is quiet. "Did you tell him that's what he should do?"

I can't bear that I'm the guy who made the worst day of her life that much harder. The end of her marriage to Chris was inevitable. He didn't want to be with her anymore and my words may have spurred him to cut all ties that night but even if I hadn't crossed his path, I have every belief that Chloe and I would be together now. Their marriage was inching toward its death.

"I told him that life is short and if he wasn't getting what he needed that he should move on." I exhale roughly. "I'm sorry, Chloe. I'm sorry that I pushed him to leave you that night but I'm damn sure not sorry that he did."

"He left the hospital before I did." Her hands knead together in her lap. "By the time I made it back to the apartment, most of my things were boxed up and sitting in the foyer."

"What a fucking bastard. I didn't know that he'd take my advice and end things that night. It's a heartless move to dump someone the night their mother dies."

"I was in shock." She slides closer to me. "I took what I needed and went to be with my dad. He needed me that night and even though I loved Chris at the time, I was too numb to care that he had thrown me out."

Her words bite through me. I don't want to know that she loved him at one time, although it's obvious given the fact that they were together for ten years.

"After my mom's funeral, I arranged to have all of my things brought to my dad's place and then eventually I started building a life of my own." Her voice quivers. "It hasn't been easy but I've done it without a cent from Chris. I used my inheritance to start my own firm and I put a down payment on this place with the rest of the money my mom left me."

"You're a strong person." I turn to look into her face. "You went through hell that night and you came out the other side in one piece."

"I did it because I had to." Our eyes meet and she smiles. "I knew that there was happiness waiting for me at some point. I just kept trying to find it."

"Tell me that you don't hate me, Chloe." I move a piece of hair from her cheek. "Tell me that I didn't fuck up everything before we even met."

She reaches to grab my hand so she can press it against her cheek. "You tried to save my mom's life and you saved me from a marriage that wasn't right for me. How could I hate you?"

Relief washes over me like a wave. I feel the tension in my shoulders instantly release. "I haven't slept since I realized I changed your life that night."

Her arms move to circle my neck as she gazes into my eyes. "If my marriage wouldn't have ended, we wouldn't be having a baby."

"And I wouldn't be crazy in love with you."

Her eyes drop to my mouth. "Did you just say you love me, Evan?"

I kiss her softy, dipping my tongue between her soft pink lips for a taste. "I love you, Chloe."

"I love you, too," she whispers back before she kisses me back with a tenderness that tells me the three of us are going to be just fine.

Chapter 47

Chloe

I breath him in, relishing in the fact that the man that I love is in my bed, in the middle of the day making me feel like the world doesn't exist beyond these walls.

I reach up and brush the pad of my thumb over his bottom lip. It's swollen from when we kissed in the living room. It was slow and gentle before his hands found the buttons of my dress and everything changed into a desire so consuming that we were clawing at each other's clothing, each desperate to get the other one naked.

He carried me into my bedroom with my legs wrapped around his waist while I rained kisses over his neck.

He wanted to taste me but the need to feel him inside of me was too much, so I pulled him on top and told him to take me.

He did with powerful strokes that drove me into an intense orgasm almost immediately. Now, we're together with me on my back and him hovering over me while he juts his cock into me in long, easy thrusts.

"Will you always fuck me like this?" I ask breathlessly, knowing that I'll come again if he changes the pace at all.

"Always."

My hands move over his thighs and he growls his approval. "I love touching you, Evan. You're only the second man…"

"Shhh." His lips cover mine to steal the word as his body stalls. "All that matters is that I'm the first man who has loved you like this. I'm the only man who will treasure you forever and no other man will ever fuck you again."

Tears sting the corners of my eyes as he leans back so he can increase the pace of his thrusts.

I feel the thick ridges of his cock inside of me as he pumps harder. "Ah, Chloe. It's so fucking good."

It's so good. I didn't know it could be like this. I try to say something back but all that escapes me is a moan, a symbol of what my body is feeling.

He holds me down as he nears his release and as I start to come, I chant his name, wanting him to know that I'm his forever.

***

I walk back into my bedroom wearing only a pair of white panties. "So I take it that you're a vascular surgeon?"

He's sitting on the edge of my bed staring down at the screen of his phone. "You've solved that mystery. Tell me how old you are."

"Twenty-nine." I sit next to him before I hand him a glass of water. "Are there any secrets left between us?"

He downs the water in one large gulp before he places the glass on the bedside table. "No more deep dark secrets on my end. There are things about me I want you to know and people you've got to meet, but for the most part, you know who Dr. Evan Scott is now."

"He's a compassionate, gifted, and incredibly sexy man."

"That he is." He kisses the tip of my nose. "Tell me about the secrets that Chloe Jones or is it Chloe Neville is hiding?"

"It's going to be Jones very soon." I snuggle next to him. "My divorce wasn't finalized until just a few months ago and one of the terms of the prenup was that I had to keep the name until the marriage was officially over."

He looks down at the floor. "I'm going to say something here, Chloe, and shoot me down if you think it's totally fucked up."

Tension tugs on my nerves. I don't want him to talk about Christopher ever again. He's a part of my past and I'm moving toward a future with him and our baby. "What is it?"

"Marry me. I want you to be Chloe Scott."

I look at him while my heart hammers in my chest. How can I marry him? We only met a few months ago. Our entire relationship has been one surprise after another. "Is it too early for that?"

"That's not a yes." He smiles softly. "I'd like to be your husband before the baby arrives. That gives you some time to think about whether you want the same thing. If you do, we'll get married."

I bit the corner of my lip as I consider what he just said. "Do you want to get married because of the baby?"

Our eyes meet. "I want to get married because I love you. I love you, Chloe and I want our child to grow up witnessing that love every day of her life."

"Or his," I correct him with a grin. "We both know that this might be a little boy."

"This is a little girl." He leans down to kiss my bare stomach. "One day when she's old enough to understand we'll tell her the story of how her mom and dad fell in love."

"You'll leave out the part about the one-night stand, right?" I question with a giggle. "You're not telling my daughter that I picked you up outside a hotel room on a snowy night."

"We can leave out some details. " He scoops me into his lap and his cock instantly stirs. "I have time to make love to you again before I need to get back to the hospital. What's on your agenda for this afternoon."

I shift so I'm straddling him.

I take in the sight of his handsome face. It's changed since I first saw him. It's no longer just the face of a man I fucked the first night we met. Now, it's the face of my partner, my friend and the face of the man I love more than anything.

"I'm going to spend my afternoon in bed with my fiancé. "

His grip on me tightens as he slides me forward along his erection. "Your fiancé loves that answer almost as much as he loves you."

Epilogue

1 Year Later

Evan

"I didn't think you had it in you, Jordan." I slap him across the back.

"What? Sperm that work?" He grabs the front of his black pants. "I'm just as capable of getting a woman pregnant as you are, Evan."

Apparently, that's the truth.

It may be my wife's birthday but Jordan stole the thunder with the announcement that he's going to be a father. Kylie actually blushed when Jordan gave a mini speech about how much he's going to love being a dad.

He will.

My life changed the day my daughter, Elena Jones Scott, was born. Labor was a breeze. The delivery was uncomplicated.

Chloe was strong. She was stronger than I was and when Rita told us that it was a girl I looked at my wife and smiled.

We never asked Rita what the gender of our baby was. We both instinctively knew.

The day after I moved in with Chloe, I painted the extra bedroom in our apartment yellow because it was supposed to calm the baby.

That benefit hasn't kicked in quite yet. Elena rarely sleeps, always smiles and when I'm not at work, I'm as hands on as a parent can be. Chloe is the same and when we're both at work, Jenny, our nanny keeps our baby safe.

"Where's your beautiful bride?" Jordan looks around the apartment for Chloe.

I know exactly where she is. "I'll go find her. Hold down the fort for me."

Jordan gives me a curt nod as he walks over to where Chloe's brothers, her dad and her dad's fiancée, April, are gathered around the kitchen table. Gabi is in the kitchen putting candles on the birthday cake.

I walk down the hallway toward our bedroom.

I hear Chloe's voice before I see her.

"You and your daddy are every gift that I'm ever going to need." Her voice is soft and low. "I love you both with everything I have."

The door is ajar, but I push it open and gave at the scene in front of me.

Warm Sunday afternoon light is filtering in from the window near our bed. Elena is on her back in the middle of the bed dressed in a light pink dress and white socks. Next to her is my reason for living. Chloe, my beautiful wife.

She's wearing a white dress and as she lies next to our daughter and gazes down at her, my heart fills with more love than I ever thought possible.

Chloe adjusts a small ribbon in our daughter's blonde hair. "One day you'll meet someone and fall in love with them and it may not always make sense, Elena, but you have to listen to your heart."

"Not every relationship begins the same way," I add as I step into the room and close the door behind me. "There's no rules when it comes to falling in love."

"Come here, handsome." Chloe waves her hand at me. "Give me a few minutes alone with my husband and daughter."

I walk over to the bed and settle on the other side of Elena, on my side, facing my wife.

"You know that she's a miracle, right?" Chloe touches my cheek tenderly. "It feels like we're a miracle too."

"We are." I kiss the palm of her hand. "It's a miracle that I found you in this city."

"I found you." She runs the pad of her thumb over my lips. "I was the one who came outside in the snowstorm to find you there."

"The first words I ever heard you say were that you weren't a coward." I think back on that day. I couldn't have known the path my life would take after that night. "You proved that over and over again."

"The bravest thing I ever did was going up to that hotel room with you," she confesses softly. "If I hadn't, we wouldn't be here now."

"Sometimes you have to take a chance." I kiss my daughter's forehead as she looks at me with her big blue eyes. She has my eyes and nose. Every other part of her is Chloe. "You did and look where we are now."

"We should get back to the party. There are presents waiting for me."

"I got you one." I slide from the bed and stalk toward the closet. "I hid it up here so you wouldn't find it."

She moves to pick up Elena before she sits on the edge of the bed. "I knew I should have snooped in there."

I retrieve the box and take it to the bed, hoping like hell that I didn't make a mistake with the gift.

I place the box next to her before I scoop my daughter into my arms, freeing Chloe's hands so she can tear through the wrapping paper.

She does in record time. Paper flies, the ribbon sails in the air until it lands on the bed and then she yanks the cover off with one pull.

I stare down at my daughter as Chloe searches through the pink tissue paper until her hands land on the square frame.

"I'm excited." She leans forward to kiss me. "I can't wait to see what it is."

Her delicate hands shake as she turns the black frame over in her lap. I hear her breath catch when she sees the three photographs lined up side-by-side.

My daughter is first. It's an image I took the day she was born.

In the middle is my wife on our wedding day eight months ago. Her hair is pinned up, her cheeks are pink and her smile could be my sunshine until I take my last breath on this earth.

The last picture is one that I got from Rocco.

It's an image of Irena Jones.

She's sitting on a bench in a park smiling softly at the camera.

There's no mistaking that Chloe is her daughter. They share the same color hair and eyes.

"Evan," she whispers my name softly. "This is so beautiful. Look at the three of us."

"Three generation of strong women." I skim my fingers over the glass of the frame. "I want you to keep this as a reminder of how incredibly lucky I am."

"How lucky you are?" She looks at me with tear-filled eyes. "I think I'm the lucky one."

"I never thought I'd meet anyone like you." I look down at Elena before I train my gaze on Chloe. "You turned my world upside down."

"In a good way." She smiles as she reaches for the baby's hand.

"In the best way. You made me see that I was capable of love." I hold the baby closer. "I didn't think I'd ever have a child, Chloe."

"I wasn't supposed to ever have a child."

I nod. "Yet, we have this beautiful human being who will grow to understand how special she is. She was born against all odds which makes her a true miracle."

"We're going to have the most amazing life, Evan." She leans her head on my shoulder. "I can't wait to see what tomorrow brings."

"We'll worry about tomorrow when it gets here." I kiss her softly on the lips. "And every day after that too. I want us to make the most out of each moment until we're old and gray and this one has to take care of us."

Elena squirms in my arms.

"I love the sound of that." Chloe moves to stand. "Every day with you is a gift and I'll never waste a second of the time we have together."

"Let's go celebrate your birthday so we can kick everyone out and I can give you my other gift." I hand the baby to her.

"What's your other gift?" She raises a brow.

I tilt my chin toward the bed. "Do you have to ask?"

She props up on her tiptoes to give me a soft kiss. "We should send everyone home now."

"Patience, Mrs. Scott." I place my hand on the center of her back. "I have the night off. I plan on spending every second of that showing you how much I love you."

The baby cries out and we both laugh.

"I'll take what I can get." Chloe sighs. "I don't care if it's ten minutes or ten hours, being in your arms is where I want to spend the rest of my life."

It's my dream come true and every day only gets better.

Preview of BARE
From the Just This Once Series

The first and last one-night stand I had ended with zero orgasms for me and my wallet gone.

I fell asleep after the man who called himself *Kent* rolled off of me and out of my life.

The only thing he left behind was a business card on the floor next to the bed.

Griffin Kent. Attorney at Law.

Since I don't know a soul in New York, I head straight to the jerk's office on Madison Avenue to get back my wallet and reclaim my pride.

I'm not prepared for what happens when I arrive at the prestigious law firm of Kent & Colt.

I doubt that the real Griffin Kent would leave a woman unsatisfied in any way. He's tall, dark haired and dangerously handsome. He's also the complete opposite of the imposter I spent the night with.

The arrogant attorney orders his assistant to help me, but he's the one who enrolls in the art class I came to Manhattan to teach.

He may be my student, but something tells me that Griffin is going to be schooling me in the art of seduction.

Author's Note: *This sexy standalone novel contains a dirty talking attorney, nude male models and a HEA the hero will do anything to fight for. BARE is part of the Just This Once Series. Each book features a different couple and since the books are not connected, they can be read in any order.*

Chapter 1

Piper

"Griffin Kent is the worst lover I've ever had." With tears welling in the corners of my eyes, I stare at the woman sitting behind the sleek wooden reception desk. "I can't believe I slept with him. I called the police. They're going to be here any minute."

She looks past me to the frosted glass doors at the entrance of the law offices of Kent & Colt. "If it's a crime to be a dud in bed, my ex-husband would be serving twenty to life right now."

I scrub my hand over my face, mascara staining my palm. "I didn't call them because of that."

"Can I get you a glass of water?" The kind-looking woman is on her feet now. "You look about ready to pass out. Why don't you sit down? We can discuss this."

Discuss what? I went to a hotel with a man last night, we had really bad sex and when I woke up an hour ago, he was gone along with my wallet and my smartphone.

"I don't want to talk about it." I look beyond her to the massive, exquisitely designed space that obviously houses a number of offices. "Where's the asshole? I need to see him now."

Her lips curl into an unexpected smile. "He's not here. He never gets in until at least nine fifteen."

My gaze drops to my wrist but the silver watch I always wear isn't there. "He took everything from me."

The middle-aged woman rounds the reception desk until she's next to me, her arm slung over my shoulder. "You listen to me. I don't know what happened between you and Mr. Kent, but there's not a man on the face of this earth who can take everything from a woman."

Great.

I'm in the middle of a crisis and this woman is on her soapbox preaching about the merit of my inner strength.

Griffin Kent took that from me too.

"I don't know what to do," I mutter to myself.

The self-appointed cheerleader next to me adds her two cents even though I didn't ask for it. "You're going to calm down and let me help you. What's your name, dear?"

I feel like I should covet every ounce of personal information after what just happened to me. I was open and trusting when I met the attractive man in the bar last night. I told him my name when he asked. He reciprocated by telling me his. Kent.

An hour later we were in a hotel room and I was proud of myself for checking a one-night stand off my bucket list. I need to wipe that list clean now and focus on one thing and one thing only.

Find some common sense and use it.

"Where are the police? I used the phone at the front desk to call them before I left the hotel. They should be here by now." I stare down at my dress. It's silver shimmer, low cut and much too short to see the light of day. I'd never wear this in broad daylight and yet, here I am.

Thank the heavens above that my parents are in Denver, completely oblivious to what their only child is doing on her third day in New York City. The move here was supposed to change my life, not drive the entire thing into a ditch at high speed.

"I think we can straighten this out without involving the NYPD."

"How?" I face the woman. She reminds me of my first art teacher in high school. That shouldn't offer me any comfort, but it does. "He needs to be arrested and thrown in jail after what he did to me."

"Were you hurt?" Her eyes scan my face, locking on my green eyes.

I know exactly what I look like. I didn't have time to shower when I crawled out of the hotel room bed, but I did catch a glimpse of myself in the bathroom mirror. My makeup was beyond repair. My shoulder length brown hair was such a mess that I used a bright pink hair elastic to tie it up into a tight ponytail.

At least, Griffin Kent left behind my clutch with the hair elastic, a tube of lipstick and my apartment keys inside of it.

Either the bastard has a heart, or he overlooked my keys as he was stealing my wallet.

"He didn't hurt me." I fiddle with the business card in my hand. "He took my wallet and my phone when I fell asleep. My watch too. He took it all."

"I find it very hard to believe that Mr. Kent is responsible for this."

Of course she'd say that. She's the first face anyone sees when they come through the doors of this law office. It's on Madison Avenue. I doubt like hell that her monthly paycheck has less than five zeroes at the end of it. I'd say that's well above the going rate for what blind faith costs in this city.

I shove the business card at her. "I have the proof right here."

She reaches to take the now tattered card from me, but I hold tight to the corner of it. It's evidence. He left this behind. I found it on the carpeted floor of the hotel room next to one of my heeled sandals that I'd kicked off before I got into bed with the thieving bastard.

Griffin Kent. Attorney at Law. It's right there in black raised lettering on the card.

If that's not proof, I don't know what is.

"Did he give that to you?"

"He dropped it," I explain. "It must have fallen out of his pocket."

Her tongue skims over her front teeth. "What does Mr. Kent look like?"

I survey the office. There's no movement anywhere. I can hear muffled voices in the distance, but I haven't seen another soul since I walked through the doors to the reception area.

Since the hotel I was at is on Columbus and Eighty-first, I walked here though Central Park. I spent the bulk of that time rehearsing what I was going to say to Kent once I saw him. I never expected to be subjected to a pre-confrontation interview by his receptionist.

"You know what he looks like," I bite back with a sigh. "I know that he spent the night with me and then robbed me blind."

"Humor me, dear." She gives my shoulder a squeeze. "Describe Mr. Kent to me."

If it's going to take that to chase away the look of doubt that's plastered all over her expression, I'll give her what she wants. "He's the same height as me, blonde hair, full beard, really nice brown eyes."

"What the hell is going on here?" The low rumble of a deeply seductive voice asks from behind me.

"Mr. Kent." The woman next to me turns quickly. "This young woman is here looking for … well, sir, I think I'll let her explain why she's here."

Mr. Kent? The voice I just heard isn't the same one that invited me up to that hotel room last night. I turn around.

Dark brown hair, blue eyes, a smooth chiselled jaw and a face so handsome that women must stop and stare when he passes them by. I know I would. I can't tear my gaze from him now.

"I'm Griffin Kent," he says smoothly as he nears me. "And you are?"

Coming Soon

Preview of THIRST
A Standalone Novel

Do you see what I see? I see my half-naked neighbor staring at me whenever he gets a chance.

When I moved into this rundown apartment, I knew I'd get used to the six flights of stairs, the broken radiator, and the squeaky floors. I didn't know I'd grow accustomed to the lustful stares of the gorgeous man who lives in the building next to mine.

He watches me when dusk falls with an intense hunger in his eyes I've never seen before.

I sense his gaze trailing over every inch of my skin as I strip slowly, just for him.

It's innocent until I finally get the chance to pitch my business idea to a trio of private investors. That's when I realize that the man who stands at his window every night with his gaze cast on me is one of the three people who hold the future of my start-up in their hands.

Rocco Jones has seen my body, and now he wants to touch it. I want my business to succeed, and I want him, but is it possible for me to have both?

*Author's Note: Although a few characters from my past books make appearances in THIRST, it's not necessary to read any of my other books to enjoy this sexy standalone.

Chapter 1

Dexie

"I don't understand why you haven't invested in window coverings for this place."

I turn to see my friend, Sophia Wolf, standing at one of the many windows of new apartment.

"I like the light," I answer quickly. "Besides, the landlord said that he'd eventually get around to adding blinds. The man is busy and I don't want to keep bothering him about it."

"You pay rent which means it's his job to keep you happy."

Spoken from the lips of a woman who lives in a beautiful apartment with her novelist husband and daughter.

"Don't worry about it, Sophia." I place another cardboard box on the kitchen counter. "I really like this place. I have a lot more room to work on my purses and the rent is cheaper than the last place."

"I can't argue with that." She takes in the large open space. "Are you thinking of setting up your workstation over there?"

I haven't given it any serious thought yet because my time is limited. I work full-time in the marketing department for a cosmetics company and part-time helping Sophia with her clothing line.

My purse design business has yet to take off but I'm working on changing that. I've put out some feelers to try and find a private investor for my company.

Supplies aren't cheap and even though I have a steady stream of customers willing to pay for my one-of-a-kind handmade purses, it's not enough cash inflow to take my business to the next level.

"I'm going to get all my stuff in and then I'll figure that out."

She taps her heel on the hardwood floor. "That makes sense."

I point at a lamp on a table near where she's standing. "Can you turn on the light? It's getting dark."

She hits the switch on the lamp and it instantly fills the room with a soft glow of light. "I have one more concern and then I swear I'll shut up."

I don't look at her as I unpack a box with dishes. "What?"

"Your bed is right in front of that window. Aren't you worried that your neighbors will watch you while you sleep?"

I picked this apartment because it's a bachelor. My bed is feet away from my kitchen and the main living space. The only area that is separated by a door is the bathroom.

I'm not shy. I've slept here for the past four nights and I haven't bothered to look out any of the windows to see if the people in the building next to mine are looking in.

"This is Manhattan." I stop what I'm doing and look at the wall of windows. "People are too busy to stare in here."

"What if you bring a guy home?"

"A guy?" I pause as I push my pink hair back behind my ears. "You're worried that my neighbors are going to watch me fuck? Is that what you're asking."

She laughs. "It's a possibility, no?"

"Not right now." I give an exaggerated shrug. "I don't have time to meet men. You can rest easy tonight knowing that my neighbors won't be getting a free show."

Her dark brown hair sways as she moves across the room to pick up her purse from the edge of my bed. It's one of my latest designs. Sophia is my walking and talking billboard and so far, I've had a few customers seek me out because of her.

"I have to get home." She shoulders the bag. "I need to make dinner. Do you want to come by for a bite?"

I look around the apartment. I have too much to do tonight. There's no way I can spare the time it would take to get to her place, eat, visit and then trudge back here. "I'll pass this time."

"I'll talk to you later in the week." She moves to give me a warm hug. "Call me if you spot any peeping Toms."

"Will do." My reply is swift. "I'm not sure what you'll do about it, but I'll shoot you a text if I catch one."

***

I arch my back in a stretch as I finally put away the last of my dishes. I don't have many, but they're enough to keep me eating at home.

I ate a bowl of cereal for dinner, taking a spoonful in between my work.

I've accomplished more tonight than I thought I would. I glance at my phone on the counter and realize that it's nearing midnight.

Since I need to be at work by nine a.m., sleep has to be next on my schedule.

I cross the space toward the bed. It's not the most comfortable I've ever slept in, but it's large and right now it's calling my name.

Just as I'm about to pull my pink T-shirt over my head and unbutton my jeans, I turn to the windows.

The building next door is close. It's an apartment building as well with dozens of windows.

Many of the windows are shuttered with curtains and blinds; the hint of light playing around the edges. A few are backlit enough that I can make out what's happening in the homes of my neighbors.

Television sets flicker, a woman dances past a window, and then my gaze settles on the apartment directly across from mine.

I know that the low light coming from the lamp in the corner makes me visible to the person standing with their back to me.

There's a light in their apartment too. It's not too bright, more of a gentle glow that casts just enough warmth that I can make out the shape of a man. He's tall with broad shoulders.

When he turns, I lean closer to the window to get a better look.

He does the same and when his gaze locks with mine, I feel a shiver run through me.

I can't make out all of his features, but it's obvious that he's gorgeous. He has dark hair and a chiseled jaw and when he slides his suit jacket off, I long for him to open each of the buttons on his white dress shirt.

He does. He unbuttons them one-by-one and as he reaches the last, he stops and leans both hands on the glass.

I hold my breath wanting more, but then he turns abruptly, walks away from the window and leaves me wondering when I'll see him again.

Coming Soon

THANK YOU

Thank you for purchasing my book. I can't even begin to put to words what it means to me. If you enjoyed it, please remember to write a review for it. Let me know your thoughts! I want to keep my readers happy.

For more information on new series and standalones, please visit my website, www.deborahbladon.com. There are book trailers and other goodies to check out.

If you want to chat with me personally, please LIKE my page on Facebook. I love connecting with all of my readers because without you, none of this would be possible.
www.facebook.com/authordeborahbladon

Thank you, for everything.

ABOUT THE AUTHOR

Deborah Bladon has never read a romance hero she didn't like. Her love for romance novels began when she was old enough to board the bus, library card in hand to check out the newest Harlequin paperbacks. She's a Canadian by heart, and by passport, but you can often spot her in New York City sipping a latte and looking for inspiration for her next story. Manhattan is definitely her second home.

She cherishes her family and believes that each day is a gift for writing, for reading, and for loving.

9 781984 161130